Woodenface

GUS GRENFELL

USBORNE

Woodenface is for Jess, Emily and Peter,
who have often been in mind while I was writing it.

The following people have all been helpful at various times
during its long gestation – Fran Priest, David Scriven and Jim
Walker in the early stages; Chris Amies, Tina Anghelatos, Janet
Barron, Liz Holliday, Ben Jeapes and Andy Lane throughout.
My thanks to them, and also to Megan who gave me more than
one chance to get it right, Rebecca, who reined me in when I
needed it and to Tessa, for her support and wise words.

First published in the UK in 2007 by Usborne Publishing Ltd., Usborne
House, 83-85 Saffron Hill, London EC1N 8RT, England.
www.usborne.com

Copyright © Gus Grenfell, 2007

The right of Gus Grenfell to be identified as the author of this work has
been asserted by him in accordance with the Copyright, Designs and
Patents Act, 1988.

Cover design and illustrations by Katie Lovell.

The name Usborne and the devices ♀ ⊕ are Trade Marks of Usborne
Publishing Ltd.

A CIP catalogue record for this book is available from the British Library.

JFM MJJASOND/07 ISBN 9780746081174

Printed in Great Britain.

FIGURES

Meg crept into the graveyard. It was close to home, but hidden from it by the looming bulk of the church of St. Thomas à Becket. The perfect place to steal a few minutes.

Other girls in the village were frightened of the graveyard. They would go out of their way to avoid it. At night there were strange noises, they said; dim, flitting lights, and so cold that if you put your hand on a gravestone it would stick there. That's what they'd been told, of course, because most of the grown-ups were frightened of the graveyard too.

Meg walked down the path, enjoying the warm sun of a June morning on her face, until she was sure she was out of sight. She wasn't frightened, but not because she didn't think the place was haunted. It had to do with what you thought about ghosts. Most of the graves were like empty houses – no one there. But a few restless souls were still below, not being good enough to have floated off to heaven, or bad enough to have been pulled shrieking and screaming to the other place. If she concentrated hard she could see them, glowing gently, hovering over their skeletons which lay stiff and still, arms by their sides or crossed over their chests.

She used to think that St. Thomas was buried in one of these graves, or in the church. But Heptonstall wasn't grand enough for a saint. "You don't get saints in the Yorkshire Pennines," the vicar had told her. Only local people lay here – Greenwoods, Sutcliffes, Redmans – generations of families who had lived, worked and died in the village.

Heptonstall church was old. The massive stones from which it was built had been quarried nearby – coarse, Yorkshire gritstone hacked from the earth. It wasn't tall and elegant like more recent churches, but its squat, top-heavy tower had withstood the buffeting winds that swept across the hills from the Lancashire side of the border for centuries. Its east end faced across the wide expanse of the Calder valley. It pointed to Jerusalem, so the vicar said, but as far as Meg was concerned it only pointed to Hepton Brig a mile below. She'd only once been any further than that.

Other village buildings clustered round it – the Cloth Hall, the Chantry House and the huddled weavers' cottages, all built of the same stone – seeming to seek protection from the elements, and from the dark forces that their inhabitants feared, at loose among the crags and cloughs that interrupted the even swell of the surrounding moorland. Despite Cromwell, despite the Puritans, the church was still the most important building in the village. Meg had been born within sight of it. Every day since she could walk, she had run and played in its shadow.

With a flick of her hand, Meg brushed her unruly black hair away from her face and fixed her gaze on the letters carved on a gravestone beside her. She had large dark eyes, deep-set, with thick brows like her father, and she had also inherited his firm mouth and slightly jutting chin. "Not a pretty child", as she heard more than one neighbour remark coolly, but then she didn't particularly want to be pretty; she liked looking like Father. He wasn't at home today. He always went to Halifax on Tuesdays, to sell the woollen cloth he had woven and dyed during the week. Today there was a fair, too, so he might not be back till evening.

This gravestone was unlike most of the others – a flat, grey slab resting on little stone legs, like a low table. There was someone below, she could sense them. She stared at the carved inscription, forcing herself not to blink, until her eyes began to itch and water. The surface went out of focus and began to waver. If she kept on staring and imagined hard enough, she'd soon be able to see through it to the faint glimmer of the presence underneath...

"Hello." She jumped. It was Dan Greenwood, the gravedigger. She knew his voice. "I didn't know tha could read."

"I can't," she said, turning round half-guiltily. "I was just...looking."

Dan took his spade from his shoulder and rested on it. He smiled, adding more wrinkles to his weather-beaten face. "I can't read much meself, but I know the letters, and I know who's buried in all these graves. Does tha want to know whose that is?" She nodded. "Well look." He put his spade down, came forward and traced out the deeply cut letters with a finger. M.A.R.T.H.A, that's Martha. P.Y.G.H.I.L.L.I.S, that's Pickles. Only her. There's not many plots with only one in. She's been gone a long time. It's 1650 now, so it's nigh on three-hundred year since she were laid to rest. There's the date, see?" He pointed to some weather-worn figures.

Meg looked up at Dan. "She's still there."

"Aye, she will be, unless someone's dug her up." He chuckled and turned to walk away.

"No, I didn't mean that; I..."

Meg stopped herself. She had been going to tell him that poor Martha wasn't at rest, but he would think she was being fanciful. He dug up bones every day; threw them on a heap without a second thought. He'd broken the spell now, but that didn't matter.

Alone again, she undid the strings of the bag that dangled from a rope belt at her waist, hidden by the long apron she wore over her plain dress. Inside the bag were her dolls – "figures", she called them. She took them out and sat them on the edge of the gravestone. There was Dilly-Lal, with her fixed smile, Drum-a-Dum with his sticks held out, ready to beat his drum, and Bolly-Bolly with his sly, knowing look.

What did they want to do? Dilly-Lal wanted to dance, and Drum-a-Dum would play for her. Bolly-Bolly didn't even want to watch. He thought they were foolish. Well, maybe Martha Pickles and the others might like some entertainment after all those years. They could be an audience. She picked up Dilly-Lal and fitted a straight stick into the hole in the middle of her back and held her out by it, her jointed limbs swinging idly.

Her mother thought Father had made Dilly-Lal, but he hadn't. He had sat on his stool, out here in the graveyard, and patiently shown Meg how to do it; how to shape the body, legs and arms, how to make the wooden pins that held them together. He'd let her use his tools. He'd said she was good at it. Very good. She'd even done the knee and elbow joints, held together with metal nails passed through from one side, and the points bashed flat on the other. He hadn't shown her how to make the other two figures. They were all her own.

"Don't tell your mother," he said. "She'd say it was a waste of time." Then he paused. "And...and maybe she would worry."

Meg was puzzled by that. "Why should she be worried?" she asked. "You carve things. She doesn't worry about that, does she?"

"No, lass." He smiled and ruffled her hair. "I can carve a bit, but at the finish up it's nothing more than a lump of wood. With you it's...it's different. You put

10

something in them figures o' yours." Meg thought she knew what he meant. But didn't everybody's figures have lives of their own? In any case, she couldn't see what there was to worry about.

Dilly-Lal wanted to dance, but she needed a platform. A low branch from an ash tree behind the grave swept down across it. That was just right. Meg sat on the gravestone and held Dilly-Lal out by her stick with one hand, until her feet just touched the surface, and hit the branch with the other hand. Dilly-Lal's jointed limbs picked up the vibration. She kicked her legs out and whirled her arms round. Yes, she could dance here.

Meg stuck Drum-a-Dum in a fork where the branch divided, so that he could pick up the rhythm too. His arms went up and down and the sticks kept time on the stretched skin of his little drum. Then Meg pounded the branch with her hand and diddled a tune. YADDLE-ADDLE UM-PUM YUM-TUM RUM-TUM, RUM-PUM YUM-PUM DIDDLE-IDDLE UM-PUM.

Dilly-Lal danced, Drum-a-Dum played, Bolly-Bolly didn't watch. And the unseen audience grinned their toothy grins.

After a while Dilly-Lal grew tired and lost the

rhythm in her tapping feet, and Drum-a-Dum began to miss beats. Meg stopped and laid them down beside Bolly-Bolly on the edge of the gravestone.

Bolly-Bolly wasn't like the other two figures. He had no moving parts, and she'd hardly carved him at all. He was made from a piece of wood she'd found one day last summer, in the field next to the graveyard. Men had been grubbing up a hedge, and Meg had climbed over the wall to have a look.

It was a neglected hedge, left to go wild – a straggly line of trees. Some were dead, held there by tangled branches and ropes of ivy, some were half-dead but still struggled to put out new shoots and leaves year by year. Hawthorn, hazel, holly, scrub oak, rowan.

The men had brought in horses with chains, and hauled trees out by the roots. But one tree remained standing; still alive. An ancient hawthorn, raised up on a low mound. It looked as though it belonged there, on its own in the middle of a field, not part of a hedgerow. Why had they left it? Had it been there before the hedge had been planted, the oldest tree of them all?

According to Gaffer – Meg's grandfather – hawthorn was a "difficult" wood. What did he mean by that? He didn't say, but Meg knew that he wouldn't have it in the house. It didn't burn well and it was unlucky. Meg wasn't sure about that. It looked hostile with its impenetrable branches and sharp thorns, but, if it was on your side, then these things could protect you. She had walked across to the tree to take a closer look.

And that was when she saw him, lying at the foot of the mound.

At first Meg hadn't recognized what she saw as part of the tree – it was just a dark lump – but when she picked it up, then looked at the tree, she saw where it had come from. There was a new cut at the base of the trunk; a raw wound caused by a single axe blow. When she turned it over, the object she was holding had a similar mark on the other side. It had been hewn from the tree.

It was about the size and shape of her fist; a knobby protuberance covered in bark – apart from where it had been attached to the tree. It seemed alive. Meg felt as though she was holding a hibernating animal just waking up from its winter sleep. It seemed to pulse and vibrate, and maybe the warmth on its surface wasn't just from her hands.

There were other things at the bottom of the tree too – a wooden bowl, a rabbit's foot and a packet of pins. Meg wondered who had put them there. She kneeled down and looked closely at the newly exposed wood of the axe cut. The blade must have been sharp because the slash was clean; there was no ragged tearing of the grain. But the surface was spattered with red blotches. Blood. Whoever had wounded the tree had not escaped unscathed.

Meg fitted the detached piece back in place, almost expecting it to cling there and regrow, but it fell back into her hands. It was hers now.

Back home she borrowed Father's tools and set to work. First she stripped the bark. It came off easily, revealing the pale wood beneath, twisted and lined like knotted rope. It was impossible to tell which way the grain went, or how it had grown into that contorted shape, but Meg could sense the power locked within it. She could see the face of a figure lurking there; a wooden face, waiting impatiently for her to give him life. With a gouge she scooped out the two dark hollows of his eyes and emphasized the twisted fissure of his mouth – a smile or grimace, it was impossible to tell.

And there he was. Bolly-Bolly. The name flashed into her mind, as though it, too, had been released by her carving.

Now she was looking at that face again, wondering why he was being so grumpy. She gazed into his eyes, waiting to see if he was going to talk to her. Sometimes he didn't; sometimes she couldn't get anything out of him at all. There was something down there in those dark holes she had made, a suggestion of movement as though some tiny creature was wriggling its way out. Then there was the spark of contact – not a physical spark like a flint would make, but that's how Meg thought of it. She felt the familiar tiny jolt in her head, the flash behind her eyes which told her that Bolly-Bolly was going to give her the benefit of his opinion.

Bolly-Bolly thought Dilly-Lal was vain and empty-headed, and Meg shouldn't encourage her to dance. He didn't think souls could see, not down there underground. She was silly to believe she was entertaining them. He thought that maybe they could sense her presence, like she could sense theirs – if they were there at all. If it wasn't all her imagination.

That was the trouble with Bolly-Bolly, he rarely gave you a straight answer. You didn't know where you were with him. He was too... Meg didn't know a word for what he was. You always felt he knew more than he was prepared to let you know just now. But was that just what he wanted you to think?

VISITORS

It was time Meg went home. Mother would be getting cross, wondering where she had got to. She put Bolly-Bolly and the others back in the bag, jumped up from Martha Pickles's grave and walked back the way she had come. She pulled open the iron gate in the churchyard wall and walked down the steps into the narrow alleyway below.

Abruptly the world changed. She was out of the brightness into a dark chasm as the churchyard wall cut off the sunlight. The opposite wall formed the back of the short terrace where Meg lived. It was windowless on this side. Only three doors broke the monotony of dark stone blocks. Her mother was standing outside the middle one, holding a closed wicker basket full of newly washed yarn ready for

Father to weave when he came back. Agnes Lumb had her long brown hair tied back, but untidy wisps had escaped the band and were plastered damply across her forehead. They were lank and straight, not wavy like Meg's. When Meg's hair was wet it twisted round into ringlets.

Meg skipped over the open gully that went down the middle of the snicket and was running with washing water. Mother was cross. Meg noticed the frown lines between her eyes and her tightly pursed lips. She was often like that when Father went to market and left her behind with Meg, her little brother Robert and a heap of work to do.

It was time to whirl the wool dry. This was one of Meg's favourite jobs.

"Where've you been?" Her mother's tone was sharp. "It would've served you right if I'd whirled it dry myself."

Meg didn't answer, but took the basket, pushed a long pole through the handles and slotted one end into a shallow hole in the stonework beside the door. It was about the height of Mother's waist – a little bit too high for Meg, but that didn't stop her. She took hold of the other end of the pole with both hands and turned it round, waiting for the weight of the basket to send it over and over, then she whirled it faster until a spray of droplets shot across the doorway. She laughed as her mother waited, trying to dodge the artificial shower and duck through the doorway and into the house. Why wasn't she laughing too? Father did. This was one of the games they played; it was part of the fun of the job. But her mother looked annoyed and told her to stop while she went indoors.

Just then Meg heard the sound of footsteps on cobbles. Loud footsteps, quick and urgent, echoing off the walls. She looked along the snicket and saw two men coming towards her. They wore heavy boots. One she recognized as Mr. Sutcliffe. He was a yeoman clothier and farmer in the village. Most of the small cottage weavers worked for him. Father used to, but now he preferred to be independent.

"I can get better prices in Halifax," he had said. "Sutcliffe doesn't pay enough. He wants to manipulate the market by controlling the supply of cloth and make a fortune for himself. I'll have none of it."

Mr. Sutcliffe didn't like it. He kept trying to persuade Father to weave for him again, but he wouldn't. Some of the other villagers were talking of breaking away too.

The other man was dressed in black, with a wide, white collar and bands, and a large-brimmed hat on his head. He was the new Puritan minister in the village, and Meg had only seen him once or twice before. There'd been a lot of talk about him. He was called the Reverend Nathaniel Eastwood.

As they came nearer, their expressions became clear. They were grim, unsmiling. They didn't look as though they were going to the church, but Meg couldn't think of any other reason for them to come down the snicket; it didn't lead anywhere else. Then they caught sight of her.

"That's Lumb's brat," Mr. Sutcliffe said.

They came up to her. Mr. Sutcliffe put his face unpleasantly close to hers and took hold of her chin with his coarse hand. She could see heavy pockmarks on his face and his breath smelled like dead rat.

"Where's your father, lass?" he said, almost spitting in her face.

Meg shrank away. "He...he's not at home."

At that moment her mother appeared in the doorway. She frowned at the men. "What is it?" she asked, hands on hips, trying to look bold.

"We're looking for your husband," Mr. Sutcliffe said.

"It's market day in Halifax. Some of us sell our own pieces. You should know that."

The minister looked slightly uncomfortable, but Mr. Sutcliffe wasn't to be so easily put off. "How do we know he's not within?"

Mother was getting angry. "Because I'm telling you!"

Meg winced as Mr. Sutcliffe hit Mother across the side of her head with the back of his hand.

"You'll keep a civil tongue in your head," he said, "or you'll spend a day in the stocks. We'll take a look for ourselves."

Meg felt like rushing forward to try and stop him, telling him he had no right to come into their home uninvited, but Mr. Sutcliffe was an important man and very sure of himself. He pushed his way in, treading painfully on her bare toes. The minister followed, but had the decency to hesitate.

Mr. Sutcliffe glanced round and there was contempt in his eyes. Meg felt embarrassed. This one room was where they worked, ate and slept. The walls were bare stone, polished bright black near the door and in other places where greasy fleece had rubbed. It was hard to keep the dirt off. The wall behind the fireplace was dull black with soot and the underside of the roof was covered in cobwebs. The rushes on the stone-flagged floor needed replacing. No doubt Mr. Sutcliffe had several rooms in his house. And chimneys. And people with the time and energy to clean.

It was obvious that there was no one else here, but Mr. Sutcliffe strode across the room regardless, past Father's loom, which took up the centre of the floor under the window. He kicked Mother's spinning wheel out of the way and blundered into Robert's cradle, waking him up. Then he wrenched aside the curtain of the sleeping area at the side of the fireplace, bringing down the rail it was hanging on.

Apparently satisfied that there was, indeed, no one secretly lurking there, he looked around the room more slowly. His eyes settled on a shelf that Father had put up above Meg's mattress in the opposite corner.

"Ah!" he said. "What have we here?" He moved across the room again and took down a wooden angel. "You see, Reverend? I told you he had the skill."

The minister looked at it with some distaste, but declined to take hold of it.

"Do we find ourselves in a nest of Catholics?" he said, his eyes wide, staring at Mother. Meg caught her breath, remembering how a local family accused of being Catholics had fled the village to avoid persecution.

Mother was frightened now, and put on her pleading voice. "We don't mean no harm, sir. We're just ordinary people. My husband copied that from one of the gravestones in the churchyard." Robert had started to cry. Mother took him out of his cradle and held him to her, comforting him.

Meg wished Mother would stand up to Mr. Sutcliffe; she hated to hear her talk like that. But the threat he had made earlier was real. Mr. Sutcliffe had the power and influence to have Mother placed in the stocks where she'd be pelted with rubbish by those who wanted to keep in with Mr. Sutcliffe.

"And what else does he carve?" Mr. Sutcliffe asked. "Does he carve toys, dolls for the children?" He tossed the angel into the fireplace and went back to the cradle. Lying in the bottom was a wooden rattle and a small doll. With a cry of triumph, Mr. Sutcliffe bent down and seized them.

"You see, you see!" he said to the minister, shaking them in front of the man's nose.

The minister looked serious. "I agree that this needs further investigation, but we do not yet have proof."

"Proof? How much proof do you want before we take some action?"

"Mr. Sutcliffe," the minister raised his hands in a calming gesture, "you called me in to assist you, and I have agreed to help, but we must follow due process of law. A man may carve toys for his children without being immediately suspected of witchcraft, I think."

Witchcraft? A cold shiver ran down Meg's body.

"Now, we are agreed that your daughter is possessed—"

"Possessed?" Flecks of spittle flew from Mr. Sutcliffe's mouth. "I've never heard of possession like it. There must be a score or more demons fighting for her soul. She throws herself to the ground and writhes her body into the most contorted and unnatural shapes. And the voices! I've counted nineteen different voices, each one uttering foul obscenities, or gibbering in language no God-fearing human being could possibly understand.

"And when she's sick...I can hardly bear to think about it. She vomits all manner of strange and disgusting materials – hay, straw, animal dung."

"Mr. Sutcliffe! Nobody is doubting the extent of your daughter's torment. I have examined her myself and am satisfied. But that does not mean we must leap to judgment as to who is the cause of it. If, in excess of zeal, we accuse the wrong person, then we put our own souls in jeopardy."

Mother was biting her lip and trembling; holding Robert so tightly that he began to cry again. Meg slunk into the corner by the door trying not to be noticed, trying to make sense of what the men were saying. Patience Sutcliffe was a mean, whey-faced girl a few years younger than Meg, but thin and sickly, always dressed in a clean white apron and a close-fitting bonnet. Meg knew she was ill again, but hadn't known till now what was the matter with her.

How could they – or rather Mr. Sutcliffe – think that Father had anything to do with it? They were talking about witchcraft, magic. Father had no powers like that. And if he had, he wouldn't go around afflicting girls. Even mean ones.

Reverend Eastwood took a deep breath. "We must be sure of what we do. We're not dealing with some old hedge-witch here. John Lumb is respected in the village."

"Not by me!" Mr. Sutcliffe glared at the minister. "First he attacks my business by persuading others not to weave my wool and not to trade their cloth in the village, and now he attacks my family. He means us harm. If it isn't him afflicting Patience, who is it, eh? I tell you, Reverend, someone should burn for this."

The minister looked grave. He took off his hat and wiped his brow with a kerchief. "This is not a burning matter. A witch may be hanged like a common felon, but even then the courts are reluctant to condemn unless...unless there is death involved."

Mr. Sutcliffe's face went red with anger and he smashed his fist against Father's loom, making Meg jump.

"Does my daughter have to die, then, before you'll do something about this abomination? Do my cattle and sheep have to perish? Do my crops have to wither in the field and the rest of my family be driven to starvation? We need to question John Lumb and he's not here. We're wasting our time." With that, he stalked to the door.

"Wait!"

Mr. Sutcliffe paused on the threshold.

"There is one way we might know if we are near the mark. I would try that before we go."

Mr. Sutcliffe moved from the door, his shoulders hunched, his thick brows drawn together.

"What is it?"

The minister didn't reply, but turned to Mother. "Mistress Lumb, I'm sure I need not impress on you how serious this situation is. I am going to ask you a question, and if you are later found to have lied in answering it will go hard with you, on earth and in heaven."

He took something out of his pocket, laid it on his open palm and showed it to Mother.

"Tell me," said the minister, "and mind you speak the truth. Is this doll the work of your husband?"

A doll? Meg was puzzled. Where would the minister get a doll from?

Mother looked at it closely and shook her head. "No, sir. I've never seen it before."

The minister gave her a long look before withdrawing his hand.

"I do not think she dissembles," he said to Mr. Sutcliffe, "but we'll see what the girl has to say." He beckoned Meg towards him.

She stepped forward, her heart pounding. The minister held out his hand and showed her the doll. It was the image of a girl with an apron and bonnet. Meg felt her stomach turn over and her face go hot. Surely the minister must notice, the way he was peering at her.

"Now, child," he said. "Was this doll made by your father, eh?"

Meg raised her head and looked straight in the minister's eyes. "No, sir," she said. "That isn't my father's carving."

It was true. The doll lying in the minister's palm was one she had made herself.

3

PATIENCE

It was a while since the men had stomped off arguing down the lane, the minister saying there wasn't enough evidence to move against her father, and Mr. Sutcliffe insisting there was. But the image of the little wooden doll was still vivid in Meg's mind. She didn't tell Mother that she herself had carved it – Mother had enough to worry about. In fact, Mother had gone to talk to Gaffer, who lived at the other side of the graveyard, and left Meg in the cottage on her own.

Gaffer was at home most of the time now. He had been a carter, carrying goods around the villages in a wagon pulled by Jack, his big fell pony, but now he carved walking sticks, spoons, plates – things people needed – and sold them to make a living. He was kind, and wise in his own quiet way. He might not know what to do, but he would calm Mother down.

Meg thought about the doll again. It was one of the first things she'd made. It had been a cold winter's day and Mother thought she'd gone to visit Gaffer, but instead she'd gone to the bottom of the graveyard where there weren't any graves yet. There was a small grove of silver birch trees with their pale, papery bark and shivering leaves – "faded trunk and fair hair", that's how Gaffer described them. Gaffer loved trees, and knew all about them. Someone had been hacking at one of the trees, probably wanting twigs for a broom or some other purpose, and discarded bits of branches lay around. She gathered most of them for kindling – Father would be pleased – but she'd squirrelled one small piece away, the little figure she would make already clear in her mind.

She could remember crouching in her clogs behind the gravestone to shelter from the wind, pulling the blanket she used as a shawl more firmly round her shoulders. The stick needed to be held tight, so she'd jammed it into a gap between the kerbstones around the grave. Then she took her knife out of her apron pocket.

It was a special knife. Father had made it for her from the broken blade of one of his, which had snapped when he was removing a kersey piece from his loom. He'd made a wooden handle for it, and a wooden sheath for the sharp end to slide into, so when it was closed it didn't look like a knife at all.

First of all she'd used the point of the knife to make a vertical cut, then peeled back the bark with her fingers. Then she'd pushed the knife halfway into the sheath, and took hold of both ends, running the blade down the stick to shave off the brown, stringy inside of the bark that still clung to it.

When the stick was clean and smooth she began to carve. Little notches first, where the head, waist and bottom of the dress would be. Meg could see the figure inside the wood. She knew what to take away and what to leave. Then came the moment when something else took over; something that meant Meg didn't have to think about what she was doing, as though an invisible force was guiding her hand. It was like that with everything she carved; there came a point in the making – sometimes early on, sometimes not until she was nearly finished – when the figure took on a life of its own and seemed to carve itself.

The little doll on that winter's day took shape in Meg's hands. She had an apron, a bonnet and a little pair of clogs peeping out from under her dress. Then she was finished, even though the knife cuts hadn't been smoothed away and the features on her face were nothing more than marks on the surface. That was how she was. That was how she wanted to be. It began to snow gently. A few flakes landed on the doll and left dark spots. It made her look as though she had the plague. Meg had hastily put her in her pocket and gone home.

The name that came to her was Alice. Alice had a squeaky little voice and when nobody was looking, Alice took her bonnet and apron off and went running in the fields. She made friends with mice and voles and shrews. She liked swimming in the river.

And then Meg had lost her.

She really had been to see Gaffer that day. He was just about to go and visit one of his friends at the top end of the village, so she'd walked with him. He could only go slowly because of his bad leg and, as they went, he had told her a story about a creature called the Skriker. It was part animal, part human, and it looked like a bear or a large dog. It could run on two legs or four, and it made a terrible shrieking sound that gave it its name.

Gaffer told her that people feared the Skriker because they thought it was the bringer of death, but he thought it didn't bring death, it just told you when death was coming – a harbinger, he called it. It was nothing to be frightened of. It had told Gaffer when Gammer was going to die. It had made him sad, but he was glad she would have no more pain.

Meg knew she'd had Alice with her then, as she'd been holding her tight during the story. When it was finished, she'd run all the way home down the village street, because she'd been a bit scared by Gaffer's story, and Alice must have jumped out of her pocket. She'd retraced her steps, but hadn't been able to find her, and wondered whether the story about the Skriker had been a warning that she was going to lose Alice.

It had been quite a shock to see Alice again, lying in the minister's palm. Mother said Mr. Sutcliffe thought the doll had been used to make Patience ill, but how could he possibly think that? Meg had heard of image magic before, but always using clay or wax effigies with pins stuck in them, not a wooden doll. Alice was just a doll, not an image of Patience Sutcliffe. Meg had made her and she had never meant anybody any harm.

And how could the Sutcliffes suppose that Father was using Alice to harm Patience when they had Alice themselves? If he had been doing such a thing, he would be certain not to let the doll fall into their hands. So would anybody. It was puzzling. She wondered if Bolly-Bolly had a view on it.

She pulled him out of her bag and put him on a stool in front of the fireplace. She could often tell straight away what kind of mood he was in, reading the expression on his gnarled surface as she would on a human face – fierce, sad, amused, disgusted. Just now it was difficult to tell; there was a bit of anger there, but he was quite excited too. She stared into his eyes. Was he going to tell her anything? She waited for the signs. There was something stirring down there, but it wasn't what she expected. She could see lights and colours flickering in the depths of his grain, then shimmering across the surface. He was going to show her something.

It had taken Meg quite a long time to discover Bolly-Bolly could do this. The first time it had happened she was playing with her figures in the graveyard, much as she had been earlier that day, and she wondered what on earth was happening when she saw moving light and colour running across Bolly-Bolly's surface. For a heart-stopping moment she thought he'd caught fire and was about to burn up.

But then the effect had settled down and she could see the inside of her cottage. Robert was crying and Mother was standing on the chair, holding one hand with the other, and there was blood dripping from it. Meg had rushed home to find that Mother had spiked herself with a meat hook when she was lifting a piece of bacon down from a roof beam.

At first Meg had thought Bolly-Bolly could see anything; a pair of eyes that could show her whatever she wanted to see, like the ball of a crystal-gazer. But it wasn't like that. She couldn't make the images come. And Bolly-Bolly could only show her things that were happening now, not in the past or future. And there had to be something of her own making nearby; something that she had given a spark of life to, as she had woken the spark of life in him. There was a little bit of herself in everything she made, and Bolly-Bolly needed that to create his visions; something to link them together. And it had to matter. He didn't just show her things for fun.

The picture on Bolly-Bolly's surface was taking shape now. She could see the inside of a room, but it didn't have the familiar proportions of her own cottage. That was odd. Where else would there be something of her own making? The sloping underside

34

of a roof appeared, but this wasn't bare tiles, it was plastered. As the rest of the room emerged she could see that the walls were plastered too and covered in limewash. What surprised her most was that it was an upper room. She could see the wooden plank floor now and the top of a ladder poking up from the floor below. Her eyes travelled across the floor and a bed came into view, first the wooden end, then a flowered counterpane, then the pale features of Patience Sutcliffe. This was Patience Sutcliffe's bedroom!

Patience was still wearing her bonnet, but her straw-coloured hair was spilling out of it as she tossed her head back and forth on the pillow. She was moaning, and plucking at the sheets with her hands.

Other people were there – Meg could hear them – and her view of the room gradually expanded until she could see them as well. Patience's mother was at one side of the bed – a thin woman, with a pinched face not unlike her daughter's, but with permanent worry lines etched into her brow. Meg watched her lean across and wipe her daughter's forehead with a cloth.

On the other side old Gammer Sutcliffe sat, rocking gently and muttering to herself. Beside her was the minister, kneeling at the end of the bed. But there was no sign of Mr. Sutcliffe.

Then she saw how Bolly-Bolly had found his way in. Lying on a small table against the wall, was the little wooden figure of Alice. The minister must have put her down there.

The minister's voice boomed out. "Prayer and fasting, prayer and fasting. That alone can help us. God grant us deliverance from this wickedness."

Gammer Sutcliffe wrung her hands and her muttering grew louder.

Suddenly, Patience flung the covers off the bed. She was breathing heavily and seemed very agitated. She began drumming her heels and fists, pounding the bed as though there were some kind of battle going on within her. Mrs. Sutcliffe grew more and more anxious. First she tried talking to her, begging her to be calm, but Patience showed no sign that she heard or understood.

The minister rose to his feet. "I think you must restrain her," he said, "lest she harm herself."

There was a cord lying on the table beside Alice. Mrs. Sutcliffe picked it up and attempted to pass one end across the bed to the minister. As she did so, Patience grabbed the cord and wrenched it from her mother's grasp, and with a sweep of her arm she sent Mrs. Sutcliffe crashing into the wall.

At the same time, a harsh, guttural noise forced itself through Patience's lips, and her mouth twisted into a vicious snarl. It was impossible to say whether the sound was human or animal, but it was filled with a violent hatred that deformed her face with ugly contortions and shocked the people round the bed.

"Unnatural strength and foul utterances," said the minister, as he helped Mrs. Sutcliffe to a chair. She was shaken and close to tears. "See how the demons tear at her and cry out against the chosen." He went on, "They cannot bear to hear the name of God."

Patience thrashed her limbs around on the bed, twisting the sheet she was lying on. There was a tearing sound as she pushed her foot through a worn patch.

The minister stood directly over her now, his face shadowed against the light, highlighting his large, jutting nose. He spread his arms wide, looking like a raven riding the wind.

"In the name of God come out of her!" he shouted, his voice hoarse and strained.

Patience stopped her writhing and was still. But only for a moment. The shaking began gently, but became increasingly violent until every inch of her body was in the throes of some terrible fit.

"Come out!" he yelled. "Depart this child in the name of God!" He tried to grab Patience by the wrists, but she struggled out of his grasp. With a cry he threw himself down, pinning her to the bed as she wrestled to fight him off. With all his weight he was unable to still the continued convulsions of her body.

Meg saw the two women look at each other in appalled silence. Gammer Sutcliffe staggered to her feet, supporting herself with a stick, leaning on it with both hands. She was trembling.

"I never thought to hear or see such things from a Puritan minister," she said, her voice a croaking whisper. "I thought we had abandoned such Popish practices. You cannot cast out demons. We must rely on prayer and fasting; you said so yourself."

The minister stopped as if he had been struck and allowed his legs to slide to the floor. He pushed himself upright, gasping for breath. Patience went on struggling for a short while, then she too quieted and lay still. Mrs. Sutcliffe covered Patience up again as the minister stepped back. He glared across the bed at Gammer Sutcliffe.

"Desperate situations require desperate action," he said. "I felt such power, and it was the power of God Himself. If I am to be the means of ridding this child of the demons that afflict her, then I will not allow doctrine, however firmly held, to stand in my way."

"The power of God?" Gammer's voice quavered. "Do you imagine it was the power of God that entered you?"

"How else would the child now be still?"

Gammer shook her head. "Surely you don't think the demons are gone from her. They're simply gathering their forces for another attack."

As if in response to Gammer's words, Patience sat bolt upright. Her blue eyes grew to the size of cornflowers in her pale, pale face. Her mother seemed to recognize this as some sort of sign.

"I fear the child will be sick again," she said, pulling a large bowl from under the bed and holding it in front of Patience.

Meg couldn't see what was happening, but she could hear clearly enough. After coughing and retching for a minute, Patience was violently sick, accompanied by a strange metallic tinkling. Mrs. Sutcliffe turned from the bed with trembling hands and showed the others the contents of the sick bowl. It was half full of pins and needles.

"Is there no end to the child's suffering?" Gammer

Sutcliffe asked bitterly, shaking off the minister as he tried to put a comforting arm round her shoulder.

Patience started heaving again. Mrs. Sutcliffe bent over her, wailing and crying, smothering Patience in a hug. The minister came round and gently eased the mother away.

There, on the counterpane, were more pins and needles, including a knitting needle which must have been as long as Meg's forearm. There was even a pair of scissors.

Mrs. Sutcliffe's crying reduced to shuddering sobs as she scooped the objects from the counterpane into the sick bowl, while Gammer turned away, hiding her eyes.

Surely Patience must be exhausted from her exertions, but Meg saw her begin to twitch and wriggle.

"Don't pinch and poke me," she said, staring into the space in front of her. "Ow! You're hurting. I've never done anything to you. Please stop. Please don't hurt me. You can have your little doll back; I didn't mean to take her. Meg, Meg, why are you tormenting me?"

4

FLIGHT

Meg froze with horror. What was Patience saying? Could she sense that Meg was watching her? Meg wasn't sure. Even if Patience had some way of being aware of that, Meg wasn't an actual presence in the room, she wasn't pinching and poking her – in fact she'd been feeling sorry for her.

Patience raised her arms, as if to protect herself, and shook her head back and forth. "My hair! Please let go, Meg. Please leave me alone." Her voice took on an edge of frantic pleading. Her arms were flailing around now, as though she were trying to fight off some invisible attacker. Then she fell back onto the bed, her mouth wide in a high-pitched scream, clutching her belly.

Her mother leaned over her and prised her arms apart. For a moment Mrs. Sutcliffe seemed transfixed, then her hands rose to her face, stifling the scream that she, too, now gave vent to.

The minister bent forward to see what had alarmed her. His eyes bulged as he saw the growing red stain on Patience's nightdress. He reached his hand forward and withdrew a long darning needle from the spot. He held it between his thumb and forefinger, examining it minutely.

"The child's life is in danger. We must take the Lumb girl as soon as possible and subject her to the strictest examination. So young, yet so steeped in wickedness and deceit. And to think that we suspected the father. There is no time to be lost. I'll gather some men together and fetch her." He turned from the bed, marched across to the ladder and left the room.

For a moment Meg was unable to move. Then the full danger of her situation came to her. They thought she was a witch. They thought she was responsible for what was happening to Patience and were coming to get her. Now. And it wasn't just image magic. They believed that Meg could transport her spirit to Patience's bedroom and torment her.

She'd heard stories of what they did to suspected witches to try and force a confession out of them. They made them walk up and down all night, sticking tender parts of their bodies to find the witch's mark – a blemish that didn't bleed, and supposedly proved they'd had dealings with the devil. The thought of it made Meg feel faint. A cold, shivery feeling started in her legs and spread up her back and sides as she tried to banish the thought of a needle plunging into a mole on her belly.

And that's what happened to those who went to trial. Some didn't get that far. A woman in a village across the moor had been thrown into a pond. If she floated she was a witch, if she sank she wasn't; that's what they said. She sank, but by the time they fished her out she'd drowned.

Meg would have to leave immediately. She couldn't stay in the village. It wasn't even safe to go to Gaffer's and tell her mother. She would have to find Father; he would surely be on his way back from Halifax by now. He would know what to do.

She paused for only one thing. From underneath her mattress she took a wooden ball. She had carved it carefully and made it as round as she could, then covered it with eyes all over, as many as she could, the corners all fitting into each other. Father had seen it.

"What is it?" he'd asked.

"It's an eyeball."

"It is, it is!" he laughed. "What's it for?"

"To watch you with."

She put it on the shelf above her mattress where the angel had been.

It was tempting to go through the graveyard, over the wall and round the houses at the bottom end of the village, so she wouldn't be seen. But it would take longer and she would still have to go down the same road to Hepton Brig. It would take the minister several minutes to come from Sutcliffe's farm – which was out on the edge of the moor – to the village, and then he had to find some men to go with him. By that time Meg would be in the valley if she went the quickest way.

She ran along the snicket and out onto the main street. It was empty, but there were people in the Stocks Inn opposite. They would see her better than she could see them if they cared to look out of the window, but it wasn't the sort of place that Puritans were likely to go asking.

Was it her imagination, or could she hear an excited babble of voices coming from the top of the village? Surely they couldn't be there already? Meg didn't wait to find out, but ran round the bend out of the village, and didn't stop until she came to a break in the drystone wall that lined the road. There was a short cut here. Steps had been laid, large stone blocks leading to a cobbled track so steep that Meg suspected even a fell pony would find it difficult to climb.

She stopped to catch her breath. A glance up the hill showed no one in pursuit. From here, Heptonstall looked like some giant, squatting creature. The church tower was its huge, angular head, while the streets were its arms, wrapping themselves round the hill, clinging to the grass and rock as if to choke the life from it. Meg had heard tales of monstrous sea creatures like this. They could catch a ship in their arms and crush it like an eggshell.

Suddenly, the place that had been her home ever since she was born was a place of threat. When – if ever – would it be safe to go back again? A tightness gripped her throat and her eyes began to blur. She had to find Father. She turned her face to the valley and set off down the steps.

* * *

Meg hurried along the heights track, open moorland on one side and a steep drop down to the valley on the other. She felt exposed up here, away from the shelter of buildings and trees. If anyone was following her on horseback, they would see her as soon as they came over the rise half a mile back. A whirring of wings startled her as a grouse clattered away over the heather. "Go back go back," he seemed to call. But that was one thing Meg couldn't do. She glanced nervously over her shoulder, but there was still no one to be seen.

Up ahead, just appearing on the skyline, was a smudge of trees. Father had taken her to Halifax last year, and she thought the trees were just above Luddenden. That was halfway to Halifax. She recited a little rhyme to herself about places on the packhorse trail:

Luddenden is a warm place,
Roils Head's cold
But when you come to Halifax
you mun be very bold.

She would have to be very bold. She tried not to think about what Patience had said, and what would happen if she was caught, but it was hard to blot out. Meg had always been taught that if she told the truth she had nothing to fear. But what happened if you told the truth and somebody thought you were lying – or wanted somebody else to think you were lying? How did you sort it out? How did people *know*? Maybe simply telling the truth wasn't enough. She wished she could see Father striding along the track towards her.

It was easy to see why Luddenden was "a warm place". It nestled in a steep-sided valley, sheltered from the worst of the wild weather. A woman sweeping the setts in front of her cottage smiled at Meg as she approached the packhorse bridge across the river Ludd. A dog came up and licked her hand. It all seemed very homely, and Meg was tempted to stop for a while. Her pursuers might still be searching round Heptonstall.

But she couldn't rely on that; they might be galloping across the moor at this moment. There was no time for a rest; she would have to tackle the climb up to Roils Head straight away. She could see the track snaking its way up, linking farms that dotted the hillside.

She passed a group of horses tied up outside an inn. Some of them were laden with heavy panniers, others were riding beasts. They stood quietly, cropping the grass at the side of the track, or with their faces in nosebags, munching oats. Father couldn't afford a horse, so he had to be his own beast of burden and carry his piece to market on his shoulders.

Where was he? If he hadn't gone to the fair, or only spent a short time there, he would have had time to be as far as Luddenden by now, or even further. It was past noon and the sun was high in the sky. What if he had called somewhere and she'd passed him? He had friends in some of the little settlements further back. He could even be in the inn. Despite her fear of pursuit she would have to find out. She opened her bag and took out Drum-a-Dum.

Drum-a-Dum wasn't just a drummer boy, he had other uses too. She held him up by the string tied to a hook in the top of his head. She watched him twizzle round as the string unravelled, one way, then the other. As he did so, Meg thought of her father; imagined him stepping out on the road from Halifax, possibly humming a tune to himself if he'd got a good price. Or sitting in one of the houses she had already come by, passing the time of day. Drum-a-Dum twirled slower and slower, then stopped. He was pointing to Halifax. That was the way to go. Father was still somewhere in that direction.

* * *

It was a hard climb and Meg finally stopped when she reached Roils Head, hot and out of breath. From here she could look back up the wide valley of the Calder. Heptonstall was now far out of sight and no one was following her as far as she could see.

A few yards further on and Meg was over the top and looking the other way, down into Halifax. Even on a warm day like today there was smoke. It hung in the still air above the town, making it look like a seething cauldron.

She had forgotten how big it was. Through the smoke she could make out a dark mass of buildings – houses, shops, inns, workplaces – all lumped together. There was no room for grass or anything green to grow, until you moved away from the centre. Then there were farmsteads and fields stitched together by drystone walls. But not many trees.

Some of the fields were splashed with colour, but not from early summer flowers. Lengths of newly dyed cloth, hooked on tenterframes, lay stretched out in the sun to dry. This was the key to Halifax's prosperity – the wool trade. And Father was part of it, in a small way. But, as he said, it was the merchants who got rich, not the weavers.

There was still no sign of him. Meg tried to tell herself there was no need to worry, that maybe he had only just set off, or was lingering at the fair. But the worry wouldn't go away; it was becoming bigger than the worry of being followed. There was a nagging at the back of her mind that something might have happened to him – a little seed of fear that was beginning to sprout leaves. She wondered if Bolly-Bolly felt it too.

He was in a sombre mood when she took him out of the bag.

Yes, he did think there might be something wrong, and no, he didn't think she was being foolish. He could smell trouble.

If only she could see Father. If only he had one of her dolls for Bolly-Bolly to connect with.

Was Meg sure he hadn't? Because Bolly-Bolly had a very strong sense of Father's presence. Was she sure he didn't have something in his jerkin pocket, for instance?

The jerkin. Buttons! Meg had made them. Father had been going around for a long time with no buttons. Mother had said she would find some and sew them on, but she never did because she didn't have time, so Meg had made some and sewn them on herself. Like Alice they were made of birch, because the heartwood and sapwood were the same and the buttons wouldn't break at the edges. She'd taken a branch and sawn little roundels off it, then smoothed them carefully and bored holes through. But they weren't like her dolls, or the eyeball she'd left at home. Could they enable Bolly-Bolly to see what was going on?

A fitful glimmer of light stole across Bolly-Bolly's surface. Meg had an impression of movement and sound – just a blur – then a picture began to resolve itself – flailing arms, a tangle of dark hair streaming behind a moving figure, breath coming in urgent gasps. Father was pitching headlong down an almost sheer hillside.

He was moving with huge bounds. Every time he landed Meg seemed to feel the jolt herself as his foot banged into the ground. He turned his head slightly, as if to look behind him, and his foot hit a patch of loose earth. It went from under him and he fell on his back, sliding down the hill, clawing at tufts of grass that gave way in his hands as he tumbled out of control. He wasn't far from the bottom now, but there was a scatter of rocks below him and Meg was convinced he was going to crash into them. With a last despairing clutch his hand closed round a rowan sapling pushing its way out of a rocky cleft. It bent, but stayed firm.

There were two other men coming down too, but more cautiously. They were shouting and one was brandishing a stick. Father lay still for a moment, then hauled himself up and picked his way through the rocks.

As soon as he reached the flatter land beyond he started to run again. He was on the edge of the town. Meg could see the church in the valley bottom and the fairground beside it, thronged with people. That's where Father was heading, but the fall had slowed him down and he was limping. The men were catching him up.

Meg was trembling. Why was Father running from these men? What did they think he'd done? She wished she could be there to get in their way, trip them up, anything to give Father a better chance to escape.

They were still shouting, and people on the edge of the crowd were starting to take notice. Meg could hear words now – "Stop that man! A shilling to the fellow who catches him." A man grabbed at Father as he ran past and caught hold of his jerkin. Father slipped his arms out and ran on, leaving the man holding up the sleeveless garment as if he were trying to sell it.

The last Meg saw of her father, he was trying to push his way into the crowd – and his pursuers were almost upon him.

5

THE FAIR

Meg stood out of the path of fairgoers, her back to the churchyard wall, glad of its coolness after her half-running, half-walking descent from Roils Head.

She wondered what to do. It seemed impossible to find Father among all this throng, but this was where she'd last seen him, so where else could she start? If only he hadn't lost his jerkin, Bolly-Bolly could have found him. Drum-a-Dum? Not much use here. He could point in the right direction, but Father might be a few yards away, at the other side of town, or anywhere between.

She would have to ask. She watched the crowd surging past. It had a movement of its own, like a stream; sometimes it flowed rapidly, sometimes it slowed down and broadened out, sometimes it formed little eddies round a particular point. But it was always moving. How many of these people had been around when she had her last glimpse of Father? Even though she had hurried, it must have been about an hour ago.

The people at the stalls and booths had been here all the time, of course, and they were always on the lookout, trying to attract customers or an audience. Maybe some of them had noticed Father rushing past, not listening to what they were shouting, not intent on enjoying himself, just trying to get away from the men who were chasing him. Maybe those men had already been asking – if they hadn't caught Father already.

She looked around, trying to decide who to approach. There was a man with a dancing bear standing to one side of the church gate, but he looked as weary as his poor, mangy animal. At the other side was a stall with a lot of brightly coloured bottles and jars on it. A tall man with a black cloak and a long black beard was beside it holding up a bottle: "Dr. Bonum's Nostrum," he shouted. "A certain cure for the ague and other shivering fits. As used by Oliver Cromwell himself, when stricken but recently." There was a queue of people waiting to part with their money. He was too busy.

There was a puppet booth a bit further on with a screened-off area for the audience, and a cart parked behind it. From the shouting and cheering she could hear, a "motion" must just have finished. When the audience had melted away, she left the shelter of the wall and moved closer, peering through the entrance.

Two lads were standing, arguing in front of the booth. They were very different to look at. One wasn't much taller than she was, but perhaps a little older, with sandy hair and a fresh, freckled complexion. The other was nearly a man; thin, stooping and pigeon-chested. His face had a grey pallor and was badly pockmarked, with deep-set, staring eyes and a thin-bridged nose. The arguing progressed to pushing – there seemed to be some dispute about money – then the thin one drew back his fist and hit the younger one in the face. With a cry of pain, the boy tried to defend himself as more blows followed, but the other had the advantage of height and reach. He took a step forward, hooked a foot round the younger one's legs and sent him crashing.

Meg was growing more and more indignant. She couldn't just stand there and watch. She ran into the enclosure just as the older one was about to leap on the boy.

"Stop!" she shouted, planting herself between them, and glared at the tall, thin young man. "It's not fair, you...you *clinchpoop*!" It was what lads in the village called each other when they wanted to be really insulting. He was so surprised he did stop, and stared at her in disbelief. What she would do when he recovered, Meg didn't know. Maybe she and the boy ought to run.

Just then someone appeared from behind the booth – a man, wearing a large patterned gown which did nothing to disguise how big he was. Under that Meg had a glimpse of plum-coloured pantaloons and yellow stockings. A rust-coloured velvet cap slipped down over one eye. Meg had never seen anyone dressed like that. You couldn't dig or weave in those clothes.

"'Sblood, Jake, what's a-doin'?" he said to the thin one as he came towards them. His voice was strange too. He certainly wasn't from Yorkshire.

"He hit me in the face, Ned!" the younger boy said, scrambling to his feet.

Jake curled his lip in a snarl. "Well you shouldn't try an' get in without payin'." He lunged forward again, but the man called Ned held him back, though not without losing his cap.

"Peace, peace!" he said. "We don't want no fightin' or argifyin'. We're brothers, ain't we? Brothers o' the fairground. I've told you before, Jake, Simon don't need to pay – he's one of us. If he can escape from sellin' useless remedies on the apothecary's stall to watch the puppets for a few minutes, why not?"

Despite his strange garb and way of talking, there was something about this man that made Meg feel it was all right to talk to him. She had been taught to be wary of strangers, but, as she'd found out, it wasn't always strangers you had to be fearful of. And she had to talk to *somebody*. He didn't seem to have noticed her, so she stepped in front of him and took a deep breath.

"Have you seen my father?" she asked.

Ned wrinkled his brow and looked at her as though wondering if he had seen her before, then deciding he hadn't.

"I'm trying to find my father. Have you seen him?"

"Might ha' done. What's he look like?"

Meg hesitated for a moment. Of course she knew what her father looked like, but it was difficult to describe him to somebody else. "He...he's tall." She raised her hand as far above her head as she could. "And he has dark hair. Like mine."

Ned let go of Jake with a warning look and picked up his cap. He must have seen the concern in her face, because his expression softened.

"There's lots o' men like that," he said. "What makes him different?"

There were many things that made Father different, but how could you explain them? Everybody was different, but the things that made two tall, dark-haired men different from each other were so tiny that even if you could describe them, how would people be able to notice them as someone went past?

"I expect he was running," she said. "And he was just in his shirtsleeves," she added, remembering the jerkin.

Ned frowned, thinking. "I can't remember nobody like that. What about you two lads?" Both looked blank. Meg could feel her bottom lip trembling.

"I'll tell you what." The man bent down to her. "Why doesn't you an' me go to the Cross Inn? All the world an' his wife passes through there. Someone's bound to ha' seen him. Jake, you go an' get somethin' to eat – an' a bottle o' sack." Jake took the money the man offered him and slouched away, but not before he

59

had given his opponent a look that made Meg shiver. "An' you, Master Simon Jolly, you'd best get back to your apothecary's stall before old Giles comes looking for you – it's the third time today you've been round here."

Simon shook his head. "I've done my stint, Ned. Let Giles Gillyflower sell his own stuff. You're better company than he is. I'll come to the inn with you – if that's all right."

"O' course it is." Ned clapped him on the shoulder, then went to ask the hot potato man at the next stall to keep an eye on the booth while he was gone.

"Thank you for coming to my rescue," Simon said.

Meg felt a bit embarrassed; she wasn't used to being thanked.

"I thought he might lay into you too, but I think we could have handled him between us, don't you?" He gave her a cheery grin.

"You're not hurt, then?"

"Not much." He rubbed his cheek where a bruise was beginning to appear. "You expect a bit of rough and tumble when you travel the fairs."

Ned was back.

"The Cross it is then," he said, and led them out of the fairground.

The streets here were even filthier than Heptonstall's, and Meg wished she had clogs on to protect her feet. She was caught between not wanting to look down and see what she was walking through, and the need to make sure she didn't tread on something dangerous, like a broken pot. Ned was talking to Simon.

"I'm sorry about Jake. I've told him he don't ought to take no money off o' the likes o' you. But he don't like that, see? He lacks a generous spirit. But he has reason – if you knew the half o' what that boy's been through your heart would melt, so it would. You can tell by the look of him he's suffered. He's had every mortal illness known to man – an' then a few more. He's knocked at death's door so oft you'd think they was neighbours. I won't deny as life might've twisted him a bit, but... No hard feelings, eh?"

Meg thought Simon was going to find that difficult. He dropped back until he was walking next to her, and his face brightened.

"Don't worry," he said. "We'll find your father. He may be in one of the inns. If not, I expect he's still enjoying the fair. Maybe he's in the apeman tent. Have you seen the apeman?"

She shook her head.

"I'll take you later – if there's time. You won't have to pay – we'll sneak in under the canvas. He's supposed to be half man, half ape, but I think he's a fraud. See if you agree."

As they crossed the street to go through the gateway into the Cross Inn yard, they were nearly bowled over by a well-dressed gentleman in a state of great agitation.

"Help! I've been robbed!" the man shouted. He took one look at Ned and ran on, obviously thinking that such an outlandish person was best avoided.

If the man had stopped, Meg was sure Ned would have helped him. You couldn't always judge by appearances. She'd only just met Ned, but if you looked at the wrinkles on his face, you could see that he was more used to smiling than frowning. And the way he talked was friendly – real friendly, not pretend friendly in the way some adults talked to children. Besides, if there was any real danger, Bolly-Bolly would have sensed it and he'd be stirring, but he was quite still in the bag.

The inn yard was bigger than it looked from the outside. Buildings were arranged in a horseshoe round it – the inn on two sides and the stable block on the other, with a mounting block in front of it. The ground was paved with large stone setts – much bigger than the cobbles in the street – and they were strewn with straw and horse droppings. In the middle of the yard a man juggling with large knives had attracted a crowd. Meg skirted round them and followed Ned and Simon up a short flight of steps and into the inn.

The barroom was low-ceilinged and dim, despite the sunlight struggling through the narrow panes of the heavily-mullioned window. There was bread and meat on the bar, which reminded Meg how hungry she was; she hadn't eaten since breakfast.

The place smelled of ale and tallow, though the candles weren't lit. It was nearly empty, thanks to the juggler, and Meg sensed the heavy, unnatural quiet of a place that is usually full of noise. Ned went over to a table by the yard window where a woman was sitting.

She was nearly as big as he was, though her clothes were duller. She wore a brown kersey dress, the cloth coarsely woven – not as good as Father's – and it was rather worn and dirty. She had a mob cap on her head, and lank, grey hair straggled out of it like wisps of hay in a winter hedge.

"This here's Nan," Ned told Meg, "a very old friend of mine. There's nothing happens in this place what she don't know about." Meg wasn't sure what to do.

"I'm Meg," she said, and dropped a clumsy curtsy like her old Gammer had taught her before she died. This set the woman off into a hoarse cackle of laughter. She leaned forward and cupped Meg's face in her hands. They were rough, and the woman smelled like boiled nettles.

"Any friend o' Ned's is a friend o' mine," she said, rocking Meg's head none too gently.

Ned was amused too. He took off his cap and gave her a huge bow. Then he and Nan had another good laugh, but it was good natured; they weren't mocking her.

"Young Meg here's looking for her father," Ned said. "And seein' as you knows everybody hereabouts, I thought we'd ask you if you'd seen him."

"What's 'is name?" Nan asked.

"John Lumb."

Nan frowned and pursed her lips, which almost made them disappear and caused her chin to stick out. "I know three John Lumbs in Halifax," she said, "and I doubt if any of 'em's your father."

"But I'm from Heptonstall," Meg said.

Ned's eyes grew round with surprise. "Heptonstall? But that's halfway to Lancashire. I'll be passing through on my way to Pendle tomorrow. There's me thinking you're a Halifax girl and your mother's sent you out to tell your father his dinner's ready."

"Oh, that John Lumb," Nan said. "John Lumb, weaver, of Heptonstall. Used to be a Halifax lad. Brother o' Lizzie. Son o' Jacob and Nellie. Both dead, God rest their souls. He were in 'ere about midday. On his way home, 'e said. Still had 'is piece, 'cos prices were bad an' 'e didn't sell. You must've missed him. I let 'im have a drink on th' slate – 'e's a trustworthy man, your father."

Meg shook her head. "I didn't miss him. I walked on the track all the way." She couldn't tell them how she was certain he hadn't gone back home.

Ned looked at her with concern. "It's too late to go back to Heptonstall now. What're you goin' to do if you don't find him?"

Not find him? Meg was appalled and frightened. She caught Simon's eye, hoping he would reassure her, but he didn't look so confident now. She had rushed away from the village, sure she would meet Father and he would sort everything out. Instead she had seen him being chased by some men, and now no one knew where he was. As Gaffer would say, she'd "jumped out of the pot into the kettle".

"I...I don't know what I'll do," she said.

Ned looked concerned. "Don't you know no one in Halifax where you could stay?"

"No. I've only been here once before."

"Then you'll 'ave to stay 'ere," Nan said, squeezing her knee. "You can sleep in th' hayloft over th' stables. You'll be all right up there."

"An' I can take you back home to Heptonstall in the mornin'!" That, so far as Ned was concerned, had solved the problem. "I expect your father's there now, and they're wonderin' where *you* are."

Meg didn't answer straight away. She wondered what her mother would think about her staying in the hayloft of an inn, but she didn't appear to have any choice. As for going back to Heptonstall...

Ned and Nan were waiting for her to say something, but Simon came to her rescue. "That's settled, then. Do you still want to see the apeman?" He had decided it was time to be cheerful again. "Or would you rather see Ned's puppet show? There'll be another show, won't there, Ned?"

"I'd like to see the puppets," she said.

Ned beamed at her. "There's just time for a hunk o' bread an' a slice o' meat before we go."

6

PUPPETS

"La-diees and gen'leme-e-en," Ned bellowed, hoping to encourage people who were hovering round the entrance to come inside and watch. He was loud in every sense – voice, manner and appearance. "Come and witness an all-new motion, never before seen, concerning the life and death of a poor unfortunate here in this very town. Halifax Justice, ladies and gentlemen, come and see 'Halifax Justice 1650'. Just about to begin."

Jake was playing a jig, not very expertly, on a pipe and tabor. A few dropped their pennies in the tin and filled the empty seats.

There were about thirty or so in the audience, but in the closed-in space on a warm evening it seemed like a crowd: men, women, children; sweating bodies squashed together on low benches arranged in a V shape in front of the booth. Meg moved a bit closer to Simon. A young man near them cracked a nut with his teeth and handed the kernel to the girl beside him before cracking another for himself. A little lass further along the row was sitting on her hands, gazing up at the booth. There was an air of expectancy.

When Ned stopped, a hush fell over the crowd and all eyes turned to the showcloth that covered the front of the booth – a painted scene showing the notorious town gibbet with the blade at the bottom, and a severed head rolling away from it. Meg shuddered. She thought about the pieces stretched on the tenterframes that she had seen on her way into town, so easy to unhook and make away with when no one was looking. And the gibbet was the clothiers' way of dealing with what they said was a threat to their livelihood. But, as Father said, clothiers stole from weavers every day – the weave's too tight; too slack; the dye's not right. Payment cut or refused altogether.

Ned pulled the showcloth aside then disappeared behind the booth, followed by Jake, and the motion began.

Meg hadn't seen the puppets when she had been to the fair with Father last year, but she'd seen a show in the village when she was younger, before she'd made her own figures. A motion-man, travelling over into Lancashire like Ned, had been persuaded to set up his booth in the Stocks Inn yard. For someone of her size the playboard had seemed a long way up, and the little figures on it seemed alive. She hadn't understood that the man was inside the booth with the puppets on his hands, making them move and giving them their funny little voices.

She knew that now, of course, but it didn't take away the magic, nor did it for the faces fixed expectantly on the rectangular space at the top of the booth where the drama was about to unfold. First, the figure of a woman appeared, then two smaller figures popped up – her children. The mother began to speak in a squeaky, nasal twang.

It was almost impossible to make out what she was saying, which set some of the audience muttering, but the words weren't really important, you could tell what was meant by the tone of the voice and the actions.

The children were rubbing their bellies and complaining, while their mother shook her head sorrowfully. Meg could imagine what she was saying – "Alas, my dears, the flour barrel is empty and we have nothing to eat." The children wailed and their mother pulled them to her in a comforting embrace.

A male figure entered from the side and the woman's voice brightened – "Ah, here is your father, mayhap he has brought us something to eat." But her tone changed when she saw what he was carrying on his shoulder – "What is this? Whence did you obtain this length of cloth you bear upon your back?"

The father put it down. He had taken it from the tenterfield, he explained, and intended to sell it. He was prepared to risk all to bring food to his children's mouths. His wife fell to her knees and clutched his legs. "No, no! If you are caught 'twill be your death! The gibbet, that engine of destruction, waits e'en now, seeking whom it may devour!" The children hugged each other and wailed even louder, while the father blustered. He wouldn't be caught; no one saw him as he stole across the field...

At that very moment another male figure appeared and flung out an accusatory hand. He was the clothier whose property had been stolen.

As soon as Meg saw this figure she caught her breath. She felt a tingle of recognition, a creeping sensation across the surface of her skin. It wasn't that she knew the character that the figure portrayed, it was to do with the nature of the figure itself. The others were just lifeless puppets, their features fixed, their gestures mechanical. Any life they had was to do with the situation they were in, the playing out of the story of the poor family, and the audience's ability to identify with them and anticipate what was to come. But this new figure was different. He radiated unpleasantness. Even though his physical features, from this distance, didn't look any more animated than the others', Meg could sense the greed and the cruelty behind them. He was pitiless and arrogant, enjoying the misfortune of others and prepared to go to any lengths to further his own ends.

This wasn't just a run-of-the-mill puppet hurriedly made by some jogtrot puppeteer between one fair and the next. Whoever had made this figure had a skill she was familiar with. It had a life of its own, put there by the fingers of its maker and the involuntary power that worked through them. There would be no escape from the clutches of this man and no possibility of mercy.

The end was inevitable, and by the time of the final scene the audience was gripped. Several figures were grouped round a miniature replica of the town gibbet, with its two wooden uprights and a gleaming axe head suspended between them. The condemned man stood behind it facing the audience. He kneeled down with his head on the block while his wife and children, weeping and wailing, were held back. A black hooded figure to one side intoned the crime for which the man was being punished, and this time the words were loud and clear: "...and that he did, on the said day, steal from the tenterframes of Silas Helliwell, kersey cloth to the value of thirteen and a half pence."

The hooded figure stopped and raised his hand. The audience grew silent and tense with anticipation as he brought it down. A drover with a bullock stood on the other side of the gibbet, and at this signal he slapped the animal on the rump. A rope round its neck was fastened to a peg holding the blade at the top of the frame. No human being would have direct responsibility for being the cause of death.

The bullock moved forward. Meg saw the rope grow taut. There was a moment's strain, then the peg flew out and the blade made its rattling descent. It bit into the block at the bottom with a thud and the severed head rolled forward into a basket. The blade was raised, and a red fountain spurted from the neck, showering the surprised onlookers in the front row. They reeled backwards, causing the bench to collapse, dumping them at the feet of those in the row behind.

There was a moment's shocked pause, then the audience clapped and cheered. Whatever they thought about the play as a whole, the ending had been worth waiting for. Ned came round from the back of the booth to acknowledge their applause, while Jake stood by the exit shaking the money tin in case some of the audience might be moved to make a further donation.

When they had all gone, Ned brought out a bottle from the depths of his capacious gown and raised it to his lips. Telltale dribbles at the sides of his mouth suggested it wasn't the first time.

"Now then," he said, pulling it away and draping his arms round Meg's and Simon's shoulders. "How would you like to see backstage before Simon has to go back to his sellin'?"

Simon's eyes brightened. "I might even escape it if we take long enough – though Giles might give me a beating."

Ned raised his eyebrows and pursed his lips. "I don't know how you puts up wi' that old mountebank. I've seen him round the fairs for years, an' he's had more 'prentices than a dog has fleas. How'd you get mixed up with him?"

Simon pulled a rueful face. "I didn't know what he was like! I used to have another master, in London."

"You've been to London?" Meg couldn't imagine what it must be like to travel so far. "I've never been further than here. I've only been out of my village twice. Is London bigger than Halifax?"

"*Parts* of London are bigger than Halifax. I had no idea how big it was either, until I got there and had to find Dr. William Challenor in Clerkenwell. It was like you and your father. I had no idea where to look or what to do."

"Will Challenor?" Ned's eyes widened and he looked at Simon with new-found respect. "Now there's a *proper* apothecary – an' more besides."

"You know him?"

"Used to, years ago, when I was an actor. Regular playgoer he was. Why ain't you still with him?"

"Wish I was." Simon shrugged, but his face said how much he minded. "Things happened and I had to get away. I went to Bartholomew Fair and met Giles."

Ned waited expectantly, but Simon didn't say any more, and Meg couldn't help wondering what the "things" were.

"Come on," Ned said, and led them round the back.

There wasn't much room in the booth – just enough for two to operate the puppets, so with three it was a squash. Not an inch of space had been wasted. Backcloths were draped from a rail at the top, puppets hung upside down from a row of hooks, and a collection of boxes and properties took up much of the floor space.

"How do you do the blood?" Simon asked.

"I don't know as I should show you – trade secret, that is. But I don't suppose you're goin' to set up a rival motion, are you?" Ned took the body of the father puppet from the playboard and upended it. Inside the glove was a small pigskin bag. "You see, I puts my hand up here, but not my finger in the head, not on this one, it's real sharp is that blade. I holds this bag, what's got red paint in it, and, when the blade comes down and takes the head off, I gives it a squeeze, and there you has the gory spectacle of blood shooting out of his jugular. That's what the public wants to see, a bit of a spectacle. We done it first in *Julius Caesar*. Lovely, that, all them dagger cuts, and the blood soakin' his toga."

Meg was more interested in the puppets themselves, curious to see how they were made. She picked up the mother and examined her. The face was glossy and painted, with bold, exaggerated features, though they hadn't looked so crude from the audience. She put the glove on, pushed one finger up inside the hollow head and another finger and her thumb into the little arms. Now Mother could nod and shake her head and wave her arms about.

When she looked more closely, Meg could see that overlapping strips of material had been stuck over the modelled head. She waggled her finger about inside. It had a waxy feel and her nail snagged on thin strips of wood, which must form the framework it was built on.

"Who made the puppets?" she asked.

Ned put the decapitated puppet back on the playboard. "I makes some of 'em myself, an' Jake makes others. He may have his faults, but he's good with his hands. That's one of his." He nodded at the inert figure of the clothier lying at the end of the playboard. "An' this here's another." He took one of the puppets off its hook. "It's Cassius, from Julius Caesar – him what stirred up all the trouble that led to the stabbin'. Cassius is one o' Jake's specials. Sometimes he'll take to a character, see, and he'll spend time on it – intense, workin' on the detail as if it mattered. I'll say to him, 'Jake, what's the point o' spending all that time and care, nobody's goin' to see it close up.' An' he'll look at me with that way of his and say, 'I'm putting the life in it, Ned, putting the life in it.'"

A shiver ran down Meg's back. The face had a fierce aquiline nose and a cruel expression. There was something about the look of it that made you feel cold inside. She didn't know the play, but, as with the clothier, she knew what motivated this man and what he was capable of doing. He was cunning, treacherous, deceitful.

Simon's attention had been caught by the model of the gibbet which was still standing on the playboard. Meg could see that it had been carefully made, with strong wooden uprights and a real metal blade. It looked like a true replica of the real thing.

"Did Jake make this?" Simon asked.

"That's Jake's work all right. Last time we was here, I told him I had this idea about 'Halifax Justice'. 'We'll do it first in Halifax,' I says. 'An' then we'll take it round the country, let the rest o' the nation see what practices is still going on in these godforsaken parts.' No offence," he said to Meg, "but they don't chop people's heads off for stealing cloth nowheres else, do they?

"So Jake goes to look at the real gibbet. Spends hours just staring at it. Then we had to stay till next market day 'cause there was a beheadin'. Missed Pendle Fair because o' that. An' all the time Jake's talkin' about the gibbet, askin' people about them who's ended their days on it. Then he finds a couple of old rafters from a broken roof – oak, like the gibbet itself – an' he makes this, real careful like. Puttin' the life in it – or the death, eh? Like I say, good with his hands."

Meg felt the same kind of coldness she had felt with the Cassius figure, but the effect on Simon was startling. He seemed to be transfixed by the gibbet. He was staring at it, unblinking, eyes bulging.

"You all right?" Ned asked, but Simon didn't reply. He began to sway slightly and Meg heard a low moan come from deep within him. She took hold of his arm to steady him, but it was stiff and awkward.

The moaning had become a whispered muttering now. It sounded like words, but Meg couldn't make sense of it. She glanced at Ned, who met her eyes, his face filled with alarm. "We'd better get him out o' the booth," he said. "Let's turn him round an' see if we can get him to walk."

It wasn't possible. He was completely rigid. Any attempt to move him simply made him topple. "Should we lay him down?" Meg asked, but, before Ned could reply, a change came over Simon. He began to sweat, and, when Meg felt his forehead, it was cold. The stiffness had been replaced by trembling, he was shuddering violently from head to foot.

Suddenly, with a sharp intake of breath, his head jerked back and his eyes rolled up until only the whites were showing, then his knees buckled, like a marionette with its strings cut. Ned tried to catch him, but it was too late. He gave a strange kind of gurgling sigh and crumpled to the floor, almost bringing down the booth on top of them.

Simon's face drained of colour and his skin took on a pearly sheen, like marble. His eyes were open, but glazed and expressionless. For a heart-stopping moment, Meg thought he must be dead. Ned was beside him, feeling urgently at Simon's wrist and neck. He put his cheek to the pale lips, slightly parted as though Simon had been interrupted in the middle of saying something.

Ned got up slowly. "The pulse o' life is there," he said. "But it's faint and slow. I don't know what's overcome him, but it's more like he's mazed than struck."

Meg's relief set her heart beating wildly, and she let out a long, pent-up breath. Simon began to stir, and he was mumbling to himself. Meg kneeled down to try and hear what he was saying, but the words were formless and she couldn't make sense of them. He closed and opened his eyes several times, and gradually the blank stare gave way to the glint of returning life and understanding.

"Meg?" he said, as he recognized her. He tried to sit up, but fell back again. Meg caught his head before it hit the floor.

"Don't you do nothin' too quick," Ned said. "I'll see if I can find a drop of ardent spirit in the cart."

Meg eased Simon up. He propped himself on one elbow and shook his head.

"What...what was it?" Meg said, almost afraid to know but feeling compelled to ask.

"It was a vision," he said, his voice slurred and husky. "A phantasm. I've had them before. It was all about the gibbet – I was watching a beheading. It was just like the motion – the hooded man, the drover, the bullock. But when the axe came down, the severed head rolled from the block and landed at my feet. I knew that face, Meg." He shuddered and turned his haunted gaze towards her. "It was mine."

A VISION

M eg was trembling and suddenly cold, despite
the warmth of the evening. She was both
repelled and fascinated by Simon's vision. She didn't
dare think what it might mean.

She hoped Simon was going to tell her more, but
Ned came in with a bottle.

"Here you are," he said. "This'll perk you up."

Simon managed to swallow a little of the spirit. It
made him cough and splutter, but he looked better
for it.

"What he needs is somewhere to sit an' a breath o'
fresh air." Ned drew the curtain aside, then came and
supported Simon under one arm while Meg took the
other and they raised him to his feet. He was unsteady,
but after a moment he could put one foot in front of

the other and they guided him outside and round to the front.

Jake was standing there. Did he know what had happened? He stared at Meg and Simon, an unpleasant smirk on his face. Meg thought he was going to make some kind of taunt, but he turned away.

"See you later, Ned," he said, and walked off.

The nearest bench was still lying on its side from when the audience had fallen off it. Ned held Simon while Meg righted it and pulled it up against the booth.

They let Simon down onto the bench, and Meg sat beside him. Only then did she notice that there was someone standing in the enclosure, looking round. He had a high-crowned hat on his close-cropped head, and wore a buff coat with striped sleeves sewn into the armholes. A wide shoulder belt bearing the town coat of arms lay across it, though the man didn't carry a sword. His face was bulbous and a large blotch discoloured one side of it. He came towards them and peered at Ned.

"I'm the constable. Art tha th' owner of this..." He waved his arm round in thinly veiled contempt.

Ned drew himself up to his full height and looked

down on the man. "I am indeed. Edward Fletcher, Master Puppeteer at your service."

The constable wasn't impressed. "Where's thy licence?"

Ned widened his eyes in mock innocence. "My licence?"

"That's reet. Tha can't perform wi'out a licence in this town, and well tha knows it. We don't want no vagrants, vagabonds an' sundry riff-raff 'ere."

Meg took an instant dislike to the man. There was no need for him to be so rude.

Ned put on a superior air. "Don't you know I perform under the patronage of Lord Servile? His lordship would not be pleased to find us discommoded in any way."

"Dunno nowt about that. Bailiff's sent me to see thy licence. No licence an' tha'll end up in gaol."

Meg was worried, not only for Ned, but for herself. What would she do if Ned couldn't help her any more?

"My good man, as I told you, we're under—"

"No flimflam! Has tha got a licence or not?"

Ned was indignant. "Of course I have a licence."

"Then why didn't tha say so first off? Where is it?"

"You don't think I'd carry such a valuable

document about with me, do you? It's under lock and key at the Cross."

The constable gave him a suspicious look. "Then we'll 'ave to go to th' Cross an' find it, won't we?"

"But constable, my friend here is indisposed, I—"

"I don't care what 'e is. I want to see that licence now!" He jabbed his middle finger into Ned's chest for emphasis.

Ned held up his hands in surrender. "Very well. Let's go to the Cross," he said, and led the way out of the enclosure.

Meg was still worried. "Do you think Ned really has a licence?" she asked.

Simon gave a grimace, though for Ned's plight or his own pain, Meg wasn't sure. "I don't know. But if he has, the constable will find something wrong with it. Ned'll have to pay him money to stay out of gaol."

Was that the way things worked? Simon might not be much older than Meg, but he'd seen a lot more of the world. They sat in silence for a while. There was not a breath of wind and the light was gradually fading, the sky streaked with red. Meg listened to the noise of the fair coming from the world outside the enclosure. Simon gripped the edge of the bench, head bowed, chin on chest, but there was a bit of colour in his cheeks now and he was breathing normally.

"Feel better?" she asked.

"I think so." He raised his head and leaned back against the framework of the booth, which rocked a bit, but supported him.

"I thought something terrible had happened to you," Meg said.

Simon gave a sigh and turned to her with a brave attempt at a smile. "I haven't had a vision for a long time. Dr. Challenor told me they always look more alarming than they really are. I expect there'll be others; they don't often come on their own. When I was a young boy I would sometimes have three or four in one day. Sometimes I couldn't tell what was real and what wasn't."

"That must have been hard for you," Meg replied. She knew what it was like to be different.

"At first I thought it happened to everybody. It was only when I started describing them to my mother that I realized other people didn't have them. She took me to a cunning man in the village. He told us I was either cursed or blessed, but he didn't know which. After she died, my father tried to beat them out of me – he said they were sent by the devil."

Meg was appalled. There were people who thought she was in league with the devil, but not her father.

Simon didn't say anything for a while, and Meg wondered if he didn't want to talk about it any more. But he was just collecting his thoughts.

"I've never had a vision like that," he said. "It was so unexpected – maybe that's why it affected me so much. The crowd who had come to watch the gibbeting were so real I could smell them – an ugly, braying mob. I've seen what they're like in London when there's a hanging at Tyburn." He sucked in a shuddering breath and blew it out again. "I wanted to stop it; I knew it wasn't right, but I couldn't move. I just watched, helpless."

"That's horrible!" Meg said, and took hold of Simon's arm, as much for her own comfort as his.

"Sometimes I know a vision's not real. Before I left him, Dr. Challenor was teaching me how to hold on to that feeling so it wasn't so frightening. But this one seemed real right up to the moment when I stared at my own dead face. I wish Dr. Challenor was here now. He wasn't just an apothecary, he was good at interpreting visions too. And dreams."

Meg understood this. "My old Gammer said a vision always meant something; they didn't just come for nothing. She used to interpret them too. You don't suppose it means that you..." She stopped, but it was too late, Simon knew what she'd been going to say.

"That I'm going to die? No. Dr. Challenor said that nothing was straightforward – you look for hidden meanings, not obvious ones. 'Simon,' he would say, 'a vision is either given, sent or forced upon you. The fool dismisses it or leaps to simple conclusions and remains in ignorance, but the wise man cogitates upon it, that he may become wiser.' I haven't had a vision since I left him."

"Why did you go to London to look for him?" Meg had been wondering this ever since Simon had mentioned it. He must have been very young to go to London on his own.

"It was the cunning man's idea. He saw how my father was treating me and helped me get away – hidden under a pile of vegetables in a farmer's cart, with nothing but my fiddle and a letter of introduction to Dr. Challenor. The farmer was only going to Colchester, so I had to make my own way from there. Four days it took me."

It made Meg's journey seem tame. "But you found Dr. Challenor?"

"Yes. He took me in and gave me odd jobs to do.

Then I became his apprentice."

They lapsed into silence again. Meg wondered what it was like to have visions and how they were different from dreams. Sometimes her dreams seemed very real; she would wake sweating and breathless, her heart beating like a hammer. But, though the feeling of the dream might last into the day, it would fade and disappear. Most dreams disappeared before you could remember them properly at all.

Simon certainly hadn't been dreaming. She thought about how he had "woken up". He hadn't been in the familiar, comfortable world of sleep; he'd been in a distant, unknown place, and coming back had been a struggle. What had Dr. Challenor's words been? "Given, sent, forced upon you". Maybe that was the difference; dreams came from inside you, but visions came from outside.

If that was so, where had Simon's vision come from? He had been looking at Jake's model of the gibbet. It'd had a strange effect upon her; she could sense the intensity of the feelings that had gone into its making, the morbid fascination with its purpose and operation. Had Simon also been affected by it, but in this more dramatic way? Meg didn't think that an object, however much of the maker had been put into it, could visit a vision upon you like that. Bolly-Bolly could show her things that were happening, but not plant a vision in her mind.

But maybe the object could provide a link to the mind of the maker. Meg remembered the look on Jake's face when she had come out of the booth. Had he implanted the vision, and did he know he was doing it? Maybe the meaning of Simon's vision lay hidden in Jake's dark imaginings.

"Why did you come here to find your father?" Simon's question broke into her thoughts. "Couldn't you wait until he came home?"

Meg had been expecting this, particularly after she had asked so many questions herself. "No, no, I..." Her misery came flooding back. There was a lump in her throat and a sharp pricking behind her eyes. She squeezed her eyes shut and tried to swallow the lump. "I couldn't stay at home, and I can't go back – not yet. I've been accused of something I didn't do and there are people after me. There are people after Father, too." Her throat tightened again and she had to stop.

Simon's reaction surprised her. He grinned. "So, you're on the run?"

That wasn't how she thought of it, but it must seem like that. "Yes," she said, and was about to tell him more, when Ned came through the entrance with the man she'd seen on the apothecary's stall – Simon's master – so it would have to wait.

"Ah! There you are," the man said. "Idling away your time when there's work to be done."

Simon pulled a face. "Have a heart Mr. Gillyflower, it's nearly dark."

"There may not be enough light to watch a foolish motion, but there's enough to sell by. I confess myself disappointed that you do not show greater zeal in the promotion and vending of my products."

Simon dragged himself to his feet with a sigh and followed Giles Gillyflower out. "I'll see you at the Cross later," he said to Meg.

"Don't forget your fiddle," Ned said. "Who knows when I'll next have a chance to shake a leg? Me an' Jake's goin' to pack up the cart now, so's we're ready for an early start. We're off to Pendle in the morning. Promised the constable I'd be out o' town by dawn, but he still wanted a crown to keep me out o' gaol." He turned to Meg. "You'd better run along to the Cross now, while there's still a bit o' light. Nan'll sort you out."

Meg was going to ask if anyone had seen Father, but of course they hadn't, otherwise Ned would have told her. She went out into the fairground. It was quieter now; people were streaming away, though some were lingering at the few stalls that were still doing business. She looked back at the puppet booth. Ned was taking down the screens. A shadow appeared from round the back, which startled Meg for a moment, until she recognized it as Jake. He was unhooking puppets from the rail and putting them into one of the boxes. Even that action seemed to have an air of menace about it, as though his ill will extended to everything he saw and touched.

8

EVIL EYE

"No news o' that father o' yours yet," Nan said as she led Meg across the yard to the stables. "All talk on th' streets is about this cloth thief they're searching for. Took a piece off o' th' tenterframes in broad daylight, so they say.

"You'll be all right up there." She pointed up to the hayloft, full of dark shadows cast by the lanterns below. Meg would rather have stayed with the comforting warmth and smell of the horses, but Nan took her by the arm and led her to a ladder poking up into the darkness.

"This 'ere's Meg," she told the ostler and the grooms. "She's staying the night. An' mind you look after 'er." She watched Meg to the top of the ladder then bustled back to the bar.

It wasn't as dark in the loft as it had looked from below, but Meg could feel tears welling in her eyes again as she walked across the bare boards to a pile of hay. She felt overwhelmed by everything that had happened. She feared for herself, for Father, and she couldn't see any way through. It was like standing on the edge of a bog in the middle of the moor. Now she was away from the throng of people there was nothing to take her mind off her problems, nothing to stop the tears flowing, nothing to stop her feeling thoroughly sorry for herself.

When things were bad, Gaffer always said, just think how much worse they could be. Meg tried. It was hard, but not impossible. She could have been caught by the minister. She could be wandering alone on the streets of Halifax. Those things would be worse. At least she had somewhere to stay, even if it was only a hayloft. And she had friends who wanted to help her.

She thought about Simon. He wasn't like other lads she knew. In Heptonstall there were the lads who went to the grammar school – and those who didn't. The scholars could read and write, knew things like Latin and how to make numbers do magical things. Many of them didn't live in the village anyway. The rest of the village lads knew how to look after sheep, climb trees, catch coneys, warp a loom. Meg couldn't imagine sitting down and talking to any of them like she had with Simon. She didn't think they would want to, and they certainly wouldn't tell her important things about themselves.

Thinking of Heptonstall made her think of home. And of Father. It was some hours now since she'd last seen him through Bolly-Bolly's eyes in the fairground. If he'd escaped, or if the men had caught him, realized they'd made a mistake and let him go, he would have had time to be home again. Earlier she'd been quite sure he was in Halifax, now she wasn't.

There was one way to find out, of course – she could look through the eyeball, always supposing that Bolly-Bolly was willing to cooperate. She had thought of looking several times before, but part of her didn't want to know what it was like at home; it would upset her too much. But now she had to know. If Father was at home her troubles wouldn't be over, but they would be different, and she couldn't think about what to do until she knew.

She sat up and took Bolly-Bolly out of the bag. It was hard to see, but she sensed an excitement about him.

95

Why hadn't she taken him out before? He had things to show her, things she ought to see.

Pulses of light rippled across his surface, writhing and swirling like glow-worms until a pattern began to form. She expected to see the familiar walls of the cottage, with a fire glowing in the hearth. She could see a fire, but it certainly wasn't in the cottage. There were tables and chairs in a room, and two men sitting at one of the tables. One had his back to her, but there was something familiar about the other one. The picture became clearer and the face of Mr. Sutcliffe slowly emerged. Meg caught her breath. A third man was in the room – Reverend Eastwood, the minister – and he was holding something in his hand – Meg's eyeball! That explained how Bolly-Bolly was able to show her the scene, but how did the minister come to have it?

And where were they? Meg didn't think she knew the man sitting opposite Mr. Sutcliffe, but there was money on the table, so they must have been conducting business – or gambling. The tankards on the table and the babble of voices in the background, suggested this was a small side chamber off the barroom of some inn.

The minister looked as though he had just arrived after a hard ride; he was flushed and panting and he still held his riding crop in one hand. But how far had he come? He came straight up to Mr. Sutcliffe, ignoring the other man.

"We have to find the Lumb girl," he said, his words tumbling out between deep breaths. "Your wife said I should find you here. She is distraught."

Mr. Sutcliffe frowned; annoyed at being interrupted.

"I'm sorry, Isaac," Reverend Eastwood went on, "but I wouldn't break in without good cause. Your daughter has had another violent fit, during which she named and cried out against her persecutor. It isn't John Lumb, as you thought, it's his daughter working through the doll. She answered truthfully when she said it wasn't made by her father; it's an object of *her* making. Our visit must have made her fear discovery, because she has fled."

"Excuse me, Edgar," Mr. Sutcliffe said to the third man. He rose deliberately to his feet, and Meg heard his chair rasp across the floor as he pushed it back, echoing the harshness of his voice.

"I thought we'd established that John Lumb was responsible."

The minister looked surprised. "That's what we thought, but it seems we were wrong. There is other evidence. I found this in the Lumbs' cottage." He held up Meg's eyeball. "It was on the shelf where you found that angel. It wasn't there this morning, and we know that John Lumb hasn't been home. The girl is to be found with all speed. I believe your daughter's very life may depend upon it."

Mr. Sutcliffe exchanged glances with the other man then spoke to the minister again.

"If Meg Lumb is to be found, what are you doing in Halifax?"

Meg jumped. Surely they weren't in the Cross? She didn't remember seeing a side chamber off the barroom, and there were other inns in Halifax. Even so, the hayloft suddenly seemed a much less safe place to be.

"We couldn't find her in the village," the minister said. "She wasn't at home, so we went to her grandfather's. Agnes Lumb was there, but said she didn't know where her daughter was."

"And you believed her? Does no one see what a nest of vipers we have in our midst?"

The minister tapped his boots with his crop in annoyance. "I am not such a fool as you think! Whether the woman was telling the truth or not, the girl could not be found. We searched everywhere –

houses, outbuildings. Even in the graveyard. I left a party searching still. But John Lumb is not at home either, and we thought that maybe she'd gone to meet her father on his way back from market and confess her trouble to him. So I set off at once to follow the road, and I have ridden here with all haste. I didn't encounter either of them, but I learned at the inn in Luddenden that a girl answering her description was seen in the middle of the day making her way towards Roils Head."

Mr. Sutcliffe leaned forwards, his face thunderous. "I'm not surprised you didn't meet John Lumb. We're on his tail. I decided to take matters into my own hands, seeing as you didn't have the appetite for it. There are men searching for him. If the two men Edgar sent out to waylay him hadn't let him slip we'd have him now." He gave the other man a withering look.

The image of the two men chasing Father down the hillside flashed into Meg's mind again. So, they hadn't caught him, but they were still after him. And it was Mr. Sutcliffe who was behind it.

The minister looked shocked. "Then you should call your men off. There are no charges we can lay at John Lumb's door – there's no point in continuing to pursue him."

The other two exchanged glances again.

"Reverend Eastwood!" Mr. Sutcliffe banged his hand down on the table, making the money rattle. "You've interrupted my business with Mr. Womersley to give some tale about my daughter and Meg Lumb – whom you have failed to track down – and tell me I should call off my pursuit of her father. What's to say she hasn't found him already, eh? Maybe we can catch two coneys with one snare."

"You can't be sure of capturing either of them!" the minster retorted. "I shall make my own enquiries. I find your priorities difficult to understand, Isaac. We should be bending all our efforts to finding Meg Lumb. I repeat, I don't think we have anything to hold against her father."

Meg thought Mr. Sutcliffe was going to explode again, but instead he gave the minister a level look, and spoke with an icy calm. "It's not that I think catching Meg Lumb isn't important, but it's not her who's stirring up the other villagers against me. I have to look after my interests, and that means Jane's and Patience's interests too. I'm not going to miss the chance to have John Lumb in my clutches. The man needs questioning, and I intend to stay here until he's taken. You may pursue the witch girl if you wish.

I'll meet you here after breakfast in the morning."

The minister turned to go, but Mr. Sutcliffe stopped him. "So what do you make of that?" He nodded to the eyeball that Reverend Eastwood still held in his hand.

The minister looked troubled. "It's...it's the evil eye." There was a tremble at the edge of his voice.

"So, what do you believe it can do?"

"I...I don't know. Exactly. But I do know what happens to those who are victims of it. They pine. And die, oftentimes. I believe this to be a substitute for the actual fascinating glance of a witch." He spoke slowly and deliberately. "I think a witch may use such an object to project the evil eye beyond the range of her actual gaze."

"So why did you remove it from the cottage?"

"To show you. And to keep as evidence."

"And what if she should return and find it missing? What if the lass at Luddenden wasn't Meg Lumb, what if she's been hiding near home all the time? What will she do when she finds that someone's taken her ball?"

The minister was more confident now. "Ha! If her evil bauble is not there she can do no harm with it, can she?"

Meg saw an unpleasant smile forming on Mr. Sutcliffe's lips. He bent forward and lowered his voice. "What if the lass can see through this thing?" He took it from the minister's grasp and thrust it right in his face. "What if she's watching you now?"

Reverend Eastwood's cheeks turned pale and he let out a cry as he pulled his head back. There was fear in his eyes. The riding crop slipped from his grasp and he began to shake.

Meg's mouth went dry and her heart beat faster as Mr. Sutcliffe toyed with her ball, passing it from hand to hand.

"If this ball contains so much power," he said, "maybe I should destroy it, eh? I'll throw it on the fire." He made a move towards the back of the room, but the minister jumped in front of him.

"No! Do you want to bring all its evil down on us? You destroy that at your peril! Besides, it's important evidence."

"Then you'd best look after it with care."

Mr. Sutcliffe tossed the ball to the minister and walked back to his seat, his eyes full of scorn.

Reverend Eastwood held the ball in one hand as though it would bite him, and took a kerchief from his pocket.

"If we are to keep this thing, then it must be covered," he said. He placed his kerchief on the table, put the ball in the middle of it, and wrapped it up.

Suddenly the scene disappeared, leaving a momentary after-image of the men's faces, before it winked out entirely.

Meg was shaking. She'd been biting her lip so hard she'd drawn blood. The taste of it filled her mouth.

She put Bolly-Bolly back in the bag and clutched it to her. The minister had two things she had made: the Alice doll, and now the eyeball. He seemed to think there was danger just in having them. She'd seen the fear in his eyes, and that made *her* frightened, because that made him dangerous. He believed Meg was doing evil magic with them, and he wanted to stop her in any way he could.

Mr. Sutcliffe was dangerous too. She didn't want to think about what he might do if he caught Father. The only crumb of comfort was that he hadn't done so – yet.

She moved to the edge of the hayloft and looked through the open stable doors into the inn yard. Tongues of light licked into dark corners from torches round the walls and the smell of burning pitch found its way up to the loft and made her nose wrinkle.

103

Loud, excited voices, amplified by the enclosed space, travelled up from people who had left the fair but weren't yet ready to go home. A mood of hectic jollity prevailed – fair days were few and it was best to make the most of them.

Meg didn't feel jovial at all. What was she going to do? She didn't feel safe any more. And Father was still in danger. They were both fugitives. On the run, that's what Simon had said. Maybe she ought to run now, under cover of darkness, away from the town and those who were persecuting her, before they took up the search again in the morning. But she would also be running away from those who might help. And she couldn't go without knowing what had happened to Father.

9

UPROAR AT THE CROSS

Meg saw Simon come through the gateway and into the inn yard. He dodged his way through the merrymakers and ran up the steps into the barroom. He must finally have been released from his duties. She wondered whether she should wait for him to come and find her, but she didn't want to stay in the hayloft on her own any longer. She felt a bit nervous about showing herself in the open, but she might be safer in a crowd.

The barroom was full. Simon was in a corner between the bar and the fireplace. He waved when he saw her, and pointed to the seat beside him on the settle. Four people were just leaving a table. Meg waited until they'd moved past her, then went to join him.

"Nan said you were in the hayloft," he said.

"I thought you might have gone to sleep up there."

"I couldn't, even if I wanted to. I can't help thinking about...everything."

He leaned forward on the table and brushed a pile of orange peel onto the floor. "I've been thinking too. I think you ought to tell Ned about what's happened."

"But I don't think he'll believe me."

"Why not?"

"Because..." She was on the verge of telling Simon just what the trouble was, but it didn't seem real; it was like something made up. Girls shouldn't get accused of witchcraft, but they did sometimes, even if it wasn't true. It had happened to a girl in Luddenden only a few months ago. She'd been put in the stocks and... Simon was waiting for her to finish. "Because... because he might think I've misunderstood what people said, and imagined everything is worse than it is, and that if he takes me home it will all be explained and my fears will go away."

"Then you'll have to convince him otherwise. He should be here soon; they'd nearly finished packing up when I left."

Meg scarcely had time to consider how to persuade Ned to believe her, when a loud guffaw and a large-patterned cloak bearing down on them signalled his arrival. Jake was there too, dragging behind with a surly look on his face.

Ned looked at the bare table. "No drinks? How about a glass of wine?" He caught the eye of a passing tapster. "Four glasses of Rhenish."

Meg shook her head, appalled at the idea. She had never tasted wine before.

"Three, then. One for Master Simon here, one for me, an' one for this miserable assistant of mine to improve his humour."

Jake stood glowering behind Ned, clearly not in the same high spirits as his master.

"Why didn't we pack up and go straight away after the last performance?" he asked. "We could ha' been well on our way before dark. Stopped at Luddenden, or one o' them moor-top inns. I wish I was out o' this poxy town."

Ned laughed. "Jake, you're the least merriest fellow I ever met. Have a glass o' wine, see if it makes you act more jovial." Jake slouched to the bar, ignoring the glass the tapster placed before him.

"I don't know how he can be so sour in such convivial company," Ned said to them. "As for me," he gave them a wink, "I have someone to see." He left them and pushed his way to the other end of the bar where he was greeted by a group, most of whom were already drunk, by the sound of it.

To Meg's surprise, Jake left the bar and came and sat with them. Simon gave him a wary look, but Jake ignored him, pulling up the collar of his jerkin and seeming to shrink inside it. His face was almost lost in shadow, except for his eyes, which glittered pitilessly in their dark hollows. He was surveying the company in the room.

Meg could see them too. So many faces, and all of them different. The hook-nosed fellow by the fire, outlined by the flames – there was a devil's head if ever she saw one. And a red-headed oaf with a nose like a shrivelled apple. The young woman behind the bar, with her raddled cheeks and huge wig piled above her head – she looked as if she was carved and painted. Carved and painted.

With a shock, Meg realized she was seeing these people as Jake saw them – he could see the worst in any face. She imagined him making puppets of them, a cruel twist of the knife to show their discontent, their anger, their greed, ignoring the good things about them. She looked at Jake's hands. His fingers were long and thin, with prominent joints and dirty fingernails. They moved restlessly as though rehearsing the movements of the knife that would produce these unflattering images.

Suddenly, he was looking at her and the fingers didn't stop. She felt as though everything she had ever done or thought or said was laid bare for Jake to plunder. Bolly-Bolly was aware of it too. Meg could sense his suspicion and distrust, feel his agitated little movements inside the bag. She took her eyes away from Jake and fixed them on Ned, who was sitting on a high-backed settle at the other side of the room.

Ned appeared to be enjoying himself immensely. He was talking to Nan, who was sitting next to him, loud enough for Meg to hear what they were saying. They were reliving past encounters.

"Remember when I was actin' in *Bart'lemy Fayre* at The Swan?" Ned said, taking a swig from a tankard, having already finished his wine, then bringing it down too heavily on the table, making the contents slop over. "I was playin' Lantern Leatherhead, the puppeteer, and there was half an hour when I wasn't onstage."

"We couldn't wait, could we?" Nan gave a gap-toothed grin. "As soon as you come offstage, you'd slip round th' back where I was, and we'd have a quick kiss an' cuddle afore your next entry!"

Ned slapped his thigh and they both laughed uproariously, clinging to each other, drawing glances from all parts of the room. As the laughter subsided, they fell back in their chairs, and the rest of the customers returned to their own affairs.

Ned's mood changed abruptly. "Nan," he said, with a hiccough, "things ain't what they was. I was a dashin' young blade, and you was as winsome a wench as ever trod the road from Yorkshire to London in search of fun and frolic. An' now? Theatres is closin' down an' I ain't no famous actor, nor you a noted courtesan. Time has caused our bellies to sag and lined our faces like the new map o' the Indies."

Nan drew his head to her shoulder. "Never mind, Ned. We'll take us pleasures while we may, an' live to laugh another day – as the saying goes. And th' sun is none the worse for shining on a dunghill."

"True words, Nan. Never a truer word spoke."

At that moment, a sudden hush fell over the room. Talk resumed almost immediately, but at a lower level. Someone muttered, "Constable!"

A group of men stood in the doorway. The one who led the way was the constable whom Meg had already seen. He had two stout fellows with him, and a well-dressed gentleman who looked angry and indignant.

"And not before time, I may say," he said. "It is several hours since I made my first representation to the bailiff. But I know how you fellows work – you think if you ignore a complaint the complainant will go away and save you the trouble of having to do anything about it. Well, I won't go away. I don't care if we have to visit every inn in Halifax, I intend to find the varlet who stole my purse."

The constable looked resigned and weary. "Can tha see him 'ere? If not, we—"

"Wait a minute," the man said. "I would know him instantly," and he cast his eyes around the barroom. Meg recognized him now. It was the gentleman who had run past them shouting that he had been robbed, the first time she had come to the Cross. They seemed about to go, when the gentleman stepped forward and peered more closely into the corner where Meg was. He gave a cry of recognition when he saw Jake.

"That's the man, constable," he said, in triumph. "He's the one who stole my purse. Arrest him!"

Jake jumped up, dashed forward and picked up a stool from another table, scattering those who were sitting at it. He held it in front of him, half-raised, and backed towards the door.

"If anyone tries to lay a hand on me I'll break his pate, so I will." The two men advancing towards him hesitated. "It wasn't my idea," he said. Then, nodding towards Simon, "It was him! He's the one you ought to nab."

Meg was horrified by the unjustness of Jake's accusation. She knew Jake didn't like Simon, but she never imagined he would go to the lengths of trying to have him arrested for a crime which, it seemed, he himself had committed. The constable's men stopped and looked at each other. For a moment they didn't seem able to decide whether to go for Simon first, or to try and stop Jake reaching the door.

"Quick, Meg," Simon said, and motioned her out of the way. She jumped up and dodged under the fireplace arch, into the space beside the dying embers. Simon grabbed the edge of the table and heaved it over into the path of the advancing men, who had evidently decided to make him their first target. They backed away hastily as the table and its contents came crashing to the floor.

They, in turn, knocked over the table behind them, scattering a game of shovelboard and those who were playing it. People in other parts of the room were on their feet now, some standing on their seats to try and see what the uproar was. It had even attracted the attention of revellers in the yard, who were trying to push in at the doorway in the hope of further entertainment.

One of the constable's men managed to grab Simon's arm as he brushed past him, but Simon squirmed free and, with an easy swing, vaulted onto the top of the bar and ran along it, kicking bottles, mugs, pipes, off the surface and adding to the confusion below. He knew what he was doing; it obviously wasn't the first time he'd been in this kind of situation. He'd learned how to look after himself in a way Meg had never needed to – until now.

The room was plunged into turmoil. Meg, caught up in the excitement, was willing Simon on to escape.

Ned had sprung to life and was pretending to cooperate, shouting, "Come down, Simon, don't make it hard on yourself," but all the while he was getting in the way of the constable and his men and hindering them in their attempts to reach the bar. Without warning, Simon fell headlong into the heaving throng below him and disappeared in a sea of bodies.

Jake had been caught, with the help of some of the crowd, and the constable was fixing irons on his wrists while others held him. People had stopped pushing in from the yard now.

"Lock the door," the constable shouted. "Don't let the other one escape."

This set off little tussles between those who wanted Simon to escape and those who wanted him caught. Meg saw one man pushing at the door; another came up, shoved him away and pulled his hat down over his eyes. Yet another grabbed the second one round the throat with the crook of his arm and hurled him to the floor.

Suddenly, as if at a signal and for no reason that Meg could tell, the noise dropped and people stopped milling around. A space opened up on the floor and there was Simon, for all to see, cowering by the wall under the window that gave onto the street.

Having secured Jake, the constable stepped forward with another pair of manacles, but Simon wasn't giving up yet. He was by the ladder that led to the upper floor, and swarmed up it before anyone could stop him. Meg lost sight of him now, but she could hear him kicking at the top of the ladder as one of the constable's men climbed after him. It broke away and clattered down among the company, taking the man with it.

What would Simon do now? Meg could hear his footsteps running along the floorboards above the bar – there must be a passage along there. Then she lost sound of them as he passed beyond, into the part of the inn that adjoined the stable block. Meg remembered a connecting door in the hayloft – he was hoping to escape that way.

The same thing must have occurred to the constable, because he shouted for the door to be opened again, and rushed out into the yard. Those who had just piled in piled out, and most of the others too, including Meg. The constable was shouting instructions, and Meg saw the man who had fallen from the ladder limping his way towards the stables. If Simon emerged, he was going to be cut off. Meg wished she – or someone – could warn him, but that wasn't possible. He was going to run straight into his pursuers' arms.

Then a voice in the crowd shouted, "Look! There he is." All eyes followed the pointing finger to a casement window above a small lean-to at the back corner of the yard behind the brazier. Meg could see a shape at the window, fumbling with the catch. The window opened and Simon appeared, like a picture in a frame. Behind him was the agitated figure of a young woman with nothing on. "Do something. Do something!" she screamed to another naked figure behind her. It was hard to see who it was, but Meg recognized the voice – it was Giles Gillyflower. "What's going on?" he shouted. Then he must have realized he could be heard from the yard, if not seen. They both disappeared and Meg heard the swishing of bed curtains.

By now Simon had stepped out onto the sloping roof of the lean-to. He ran down the slates, flexing his knees and preparing to jump as he reached the bottom. Meg had inched her way along the wall and was now standing close by; if Simon landed squarely, he might reach the gateway and be into town before the constable could catch him.

But there, warming his back at the brazier, was the biggest man Meg had ever seen. He was wearing a scuffed leather apron and had the hot-metal-and-sweat smell of a blacksmith. As Simon sprang, the constable shouted, "Stop that lad!" and the blacksmith seized Simon's hand almost before his feet hit the ground.

Meg saw Simon flinch with pain, and his face turned white as he fell to his knees. The blacksmith's hand was huge and totally enclosed Simon's; he must have a grip of iron. He had big, blunt features, reddened by the heat of his craft, and looked at Simon with a kind of slow surprise.

"I didn't do it!" Simon panted. "Let me go. You don't want me to end up in gaol, do you?"

The giant gave a guttural grunt, and opened his mouth in a gurgling laugh. Meg could see, between rotten stumps of teeth, that the man had no tongue. One of his friends called to the constable. "We've got 'im! Big Hal's got 'im!"

Most of the crowd were shouting for the blacksmith to let Simon go, but it was too late now. A space had formed around them, and the constable, pushing onlookers aside, strode up to Simon with a look of triumph on his face.

"Not such a rake-hell, this 'un," he called back to his men, who were holding Jake where the circle had parted. "Nobbut a lad, though no doubt he thinks hissel' a modish blade." He laughed and fixed the manacles firmly on Simon's wrists.

10

REVELATIONS IN THE HAYLOFT

Meg felt angry and upset. What was happening to Simon wasn't fair, surely there was *something* she could do to help him? Before she'd thought of anything, Ned pushed his way forward until he was face to face with the constable.

"He's innocent!" he shouted. "He hadn't nothin' to do with it. He's just a young cove what's workin' the 'pothecary's stall. Jake never meant it when he said it was his idea. He panicked, did Jake. Surprised by the accusation, you see, an' he just says the first thing what come to him. Go on, Jake. Tell the constable you didn't mean it."

Jake stood glowering sullenly, and said nothing.

"Search the boy if you don't believe me," Ned said.

"I guarantees you won't find nothin' on him."

"We'll search 'em both," the constable said, pushing Ned away and raising Simon's arms roughly against the wall while he ran his hands over him and examined his clothes for hidden pockets.

The other two were trying to search Jake, but he resisted, swinging his manacled arms around, struggling and cursing. Meg guessed why, and, sure enough, once they had managed to pin his arms to his side and make a thorough search, one of the men gave a cry of success.

"Ah! What have we here?" He pulled out a purse from the depths of Jake's doublet and handed it to the constable, who passed it in turn to the gentleman, who was standing at the edge of the circle, trying to look dignified.

"Is this thy purse?" the constable asked.

"It certainly is," the man replied. He opened it and checked the contents. "And nothing is missing."

"You see?" said Ned. "The boy didn't have nothin' to do with it, and the gentleman's got his purse back, to boot. There ain't no need for you to hold young Simon no longer. No witnesses, no evidence, just a hasty word from my assistant in his extremity – and I knows you to be a fair-minded man." Meg caught the look that passed between them.

Ned held the constable's gaze until he unlocked Simon's manacles and, reluctantly, let him go before concentrating his attention on Jake.

"We'll take this 'un to th' gaol," he said, "and see what th' court has to say about him in th' morning."

By the time Meg had scrambled up the ladder back to the hayloft, the commotion in the yard had died down a little. That particular piece of excitement was over, though some of the crowd had followed the constable, no doubt keen to see Jake thrown into gaol, or wondering if he might try to make a break for freedom.

Simon clambered after her and flung himself down on the hay, while Ned hung the lamp he had brought from the stable on a hook in one of the low beams. Then he took his cap off and threw it in the air, catching it as it came down.

"Hurrah to that, says I. A close shave an' no mistake. I thought you was bound for the lock-up, young Simon. It's bad enough the guilty should go to gaol, let alone the innocent. Have you ever been to gaol?"

Simon gave his grin again and shook his head. "Not quite, though I've had a few other close shaves."

"Well, let's hope you never do – though maybe that's too much to expect. You see how easy it is for us fairground folk to find ourselves in the hands o' the constable. If me an' him hadn't had dealings before, he'd ha' carted you off along o' Jake."

"Why didn't you try to release Jake?" Simon asked, as Ned pulled a wooden box from the back of the loft and sat on it.

"Wasn't no point. He'd condemned hisself already when he tried to put it onto you, and then they found the purse on him."

"But the gentleman got it back."

"Don't make no matter. All them witnesses seen it – the constable couldn't let him off as well, could he? Best to keep quiet about that. More chance of him letting *you* go."

"Did you know Jake had the purse?"

"No. But I can't say as I'm surprised. It ain't the first time. I'll see if I can get him off later. Maybe the gaoler can be persuaded – an' that won't be the first time either."

Meg didn't seem to be part of the conversation, so she took her figures out of the bag. She picked up Dilly-Lal and twirled her arm round with a finger, wondering if she would like to do a dance to celebrate

Simon's escape. She might find that more exciting than entertaining ghosts.

"What's this then?" Ned had noticed her. "Can I have a look at your doll?" Meg passed Dilly-Lal over. "What's his name then?"

Meg was indignant. "It's not a him, it's a her. She's called Dilly-Lal."

"Sorry. I can see that now." Ned looked at Dilly-Lal closely, examining her joints and knocking her legs round. "It's a long time since I seen a dancin' doll like this. Who made her for you?"

Meg was even more indignant. "Nobody made her for me; I made her myself."

Ned raised his eyebrows and gave her a long look. "That's a skill you got an' no mistake. To make a doll as clever as this. Give her a lick o' paint an' she could dance on my playboard." He jiggled Dilly-Lal up and down on the floor. "An' not only clever. I can carve – it's been part o' my job since I became a motion-man; give me a piece o' wood an' I'll make a puppet out of it. But, like I say, it's only a lump o' wood in the end. But this?" He lifted Dilly-Lal up again and stared at her with wonder. "It's different. It's got the life in it."

Then Bolly-Bolly caught his eye. He lifted him up and passed Dilly-Lal back to Meg. "What's this one do?" He leaned forward on his box and looked intently at Meg.

"Bolly-Bolly? He shows me things and tells me things."

She'd said this before, to one or two people who'd seen him and asked. They'd smiled, nodded and said "Does he?" in that wide-eyed exaggerated way that some grown-ups had when they pretended to take you seriously, but really they thought it was make-believe. Meg was happy with that; she hadn't even told a lie. Only Gaffer and Father took her seriously, and they didn't talk about it.

Ned didn't smile or nod. He did say "Does he?" but in a very different tone of voice – thoughtful and concerned. He ran his hands over Bolly-Bolly's grain, looking carefully at the details Meg had added to his original shape.

"Where'd you find him?"

"In the church field beside a hawthorn tree. Somebody had cut him off. They'd chopped him off right at the bottom, half in and half out of the earth."

Ned peered at Bolly-Bolly's cut surface more closely. "An' you knew he was there from the first moment you saw him?"

"I found him then I made him," Meg replied.

"Twice born, twice begotten. Brought to life again." There was a touch of awe in Ned's voice. "You didn't just put the life in this one, you *discovered* it. You knew there was power there, didn't you? Only a Maker can do that."

"A Maker?" Meg felt a strange tremor inside her.

"Maybe you ain't heard the word used in that way before. Not many people knows what a Maker is; they tend to get lumped in with witches, wizards an' such like. But your Makers have particular skills an' powers, an' it's the way they work 'em together what makes it special, see?"

Some of this reminded her of what Father had said to her, though he had never called her a Maker. But Meg instantly knew that Ned was right. She felt a sense of relief. It was like suffering from a mystery illness and then being told what it was. You had a name; something to hold on to – though it didn't mean you wouldn't suffer from it.

Being different was exciting, but it was scary too. Maybe Father – and Gaffer – knew, but she could understand why they wouldn't tell anyone – even her. They would know there was a danger of people in the village getting the wrong idea about her – which was precisely what had happened.

Ned was still looking at Bolly-Bolly.

"It takes a Maker to go deep, to see what others can't," he said. "Without you that life would ha' stayed locked away like it had been for hundreds o' years. An' it's old, right enough. That piece could've growed from a seed from a tree what was growin' when Jesus was a boy. An' that's not the start of it, oh no. Go back far enough an' there's been hawthorns straddlin' over these hillsides since before there was men to see 'em, when only the Ancients inhabited the land, an' the trees an' the stones sucked in their magic like a sponge soaks up water."

"The Ancients?" Simon broke in. "Dr. Challenor used to talk about the Ancients."

"Well, he would. He'd know more about 'em than me. He's a man o' great wisdom, Will Challenor. An' Meg here knows about 'em too – not with her mind, but with every bit of her body. She sees that piece o' hawthorn and knows it for what it is, even though she can't put a name to it, and she's never heard o' the Ancients."

He held Bolly-Bolly up to see him better in the lamplight. "It's a Woodenface. Sometimes they'll come out as a carved head, sometimes as a mask, but it takes a Maker to recognize 'em. Meg does a bit

125

o' work on it, an' she makes it hers. She's captured the magic, the spirit life inside it. She can call on it whenever she wants. It takes a special kind o' Maker to do that. An' she ain't discovered the half of it yet."

"Jake's a Maker too, isn't he?" Meg said, appalled at the thought.

Simon was horrified. "Jake?"

"Yes – but they ain't all the same." Ned was quick to reassure them. "Like witches, like any walk o' life, there's good Makers an' bad. With Jake it comes from inside – dreams, nightmares, demons. They've got to find some way out. If they didn't, they'd destroy him."

When she thought back to the puppet booth, Meg wasn't surprised by what Ned said, though she didn't like the idea of Jake being given the same name as herself – even if they weren't "all the same". She could well believe there were demons inside Jake – though not the sort of demons Mr. Sutcliffe claimed were tormenting Patience. Those demons, if they existed at all, made her physically ill, but Jake's demons gnawed away inside him like maggots in an apple. If he couldn't get rid of them, then maybe they would destroy him, in time. But if he *did* let them out, what then? Could they destroy others?

"Who else knows about Bolly-Bolly?" Ned asked her.

"Father, Gaffer and a few people from the village."

"Don't you show him to nobody else, you hear? Keep him to yourself. He's your secret. I won't tell nobody about him, and Simon won't, will you?"

"No," Simon said, shaking his head and looking at Meg as if she'd suddenly become a different person.

Ned leaned further forward, and dropped his voice. "There's a power there, deep inside, and the fewer people knows about it the better. There's some would recognize that power and want to try and stop it – or rather the person what's usin' it. Like I say, there's those what mix it up with witchcraft. We doesn't want no one accusin' Meg o' witchcraft, do we?"

Meg felt a lump come to her throat again.

"It's too late," she said. "They already have."

Ned stared at her for a moment, then pulled her to him in a rough, protective hug, nearly stifling her in the musty folds of his vast cloak. She could even feel his heart beating. "I'm sorry, Meg, really I am," he said. Then he held her at arm's length and looked her straight in the eye. "Who's doin' this accusin', then?"

Simon shuffled nearer to her. He'd said she ought to tell Ned what was troubling her and now she would have to, though she hadn't meant it to happen this way. It had just slipped out. But now she knew he would believe her.

"It's Patience Sutcliffe, a girl in the village," she said, just managing to keep her voice under control. "She found a little doll of mine, and she says I'm using it to make her ill."

"Why would she say that?"

"I don't know! Mr. Sutcliffe said it was Father that was doing it, but Patience said it was me, and Mr. Sutcliffe's *still* after Father. He's in Halifax looking for him now."

"How d'you know that?"

Meg hesitated, but only for a moment – there were no secrets from Ned and Simon now. "Bolly-Bolly showed me. Just before you came earlier. Mr. Sutcliffe's in one of the inns with a man called Edgar Womersley. The minister was there too, looking for me, and..." It was all too much. Her throat was tight, she could feel tears welling up again and out came a juddering sob. With an effort, she managed to tell them the rest of what she had seen.

Ned stood up. "I'd best go an' find Sutcliffe an' Womersley. Shouldn't be too difficult to track 'em down – there ain't *that* many inns in Halifax."

"But that'll put you in danger." Meg was concerned for Ned now.

"Don't worry. I ain't goin' as myself." He pulled his cloak aside and took a long-haired wig out of an inside pocket. "I played all the women's parts when I was a boy. You should ha' seen my Lady Macbeth!" He put the wig on. "You never knows in this game when you might have to leave town in a hurry, unrecognized. I always keeps a pannier o' clothes in case the need arises. They're useful for a spot o' beggin' when times is hard, too. I'll go an' change now – an' when you sees an old woman crossin' the yard, just remember it's Nan's sister! Let's see what she can find out."

Meg was glad that she had shared her secret with Simon and Ned. Father still had to be found, but now she had help to do it.

11

IN THE GAOL

Ned came out of the Old Cock yard, cursing his luck. This was where the men had been, but he'd missed them, and nobody seemed to know where they'd gone or what their business was. Still, while he was in disguise there was one other thing he could do. It was time for Jake to have a visit from his old mother.

He picked up his voluminous skirts in practised fashion, and set off for the gaol. The looming silhouette of Halifax's unique instrument of death – its "efficient engine" – appeared further up the hillside as he rounded the corner at Woolshops. Even from this distance it had a brooding, powerful presence; a stark warning to those who might be tempted to help themselves from the tenterframes, of what the consequences might be.

Remembering Nan's instructions, he made his way through the jumble of snickets and ginnels between Woolshops and Gaol Lane. Old, timber-framed houses lurched towards each other and stopped, tottering, only a handshake away. Superseded by the fashion for stone, they were left neglected and bereft on the edge of things. Ned knew that life still stirred within them, but not the sort you would like to meet at night. He hurried on.

Like the exhalation of some foul monster, he smelled the gaol before it came into view. Then he saw where the stench came from – a small grating that was the only source of light and air to the dismal cell beneath. The door further along was pitted and scarred, as though, unaccountably, malefactors who had escaped arrest had been clamouring to get in. Ned knocked lightly and hunched himself up. He was a timid old woman come to beg a favour. He knocked again, and a third time before he heard the sound of shuffling footsteps and clanking keys.

The viewing shutter opened an inch, but no face appeared. A cautious man, the gaoler; obviously wanted to make sure he wasn't going to be gazing into the mouth of a blunderbuss.

"Who is it?" The voice was surly and thick with drink.

"Only a poor woman, your honour," Ned put on his wheedling voice, "come with a request to see one of your prisoners, if you'd be so kind."

A bloodshot eye appeared at the hole. "I can't let any old riff-raff in here. You need permission. Go away," the voice said, and the hole slammed shut.

Ned wasn't to be deterred so easily. He knocked again. The hole opened a little. He put a sixpence in the slit, taking the precaution of hanging on to it. It was pushed away and the hole shut again. Another knock; another slit. He put a shilling in this time, and felt the grasp of a thumb and finger from the other side. He pulled the coin away quickly.

"I'm sorry, your honour, but there are those who would rob a poor, defenceless woman, believe it or not, and not having seen your worship's face, I'm in no position to judge what a kindly man you might be. If you would but open the door, I'd gladly give you this shillin' – and maybe something else!" he added with heavy innuendo.

There was the sound of keys grating in locks, and the door creaked open to reveal a large man with a purple-veined nose and red blotches on his face. He was holding his keys in one hand and a bottle of sack in the other. Swellings on his neck suggested he might be coming down with the king's evil. He peered at Ned, and recoiled at the sight.

"Keep thyself to thyself, missus, I don't want no favours off o' thee! It'll be another shillin' to get out again."

Ned gave him a gap-toothed grin. "Bless you, sir, I can see you're a man of compassion. It's my son, you see. First time in trouble, and it's all a mistake. Falsely accused he was. He must be sufferin' somethin' terrible."

"That miserable pock-faced youth, is it?"

"Spare a mother's feelings, sir. He may not be much to look at, but he's all I've got."

The gaoler led the way down the steps, along the dank, slimy corridor, and unlocked the door to the cell. The place was hot and crowded and the noisome odour, so much worse inside than out, made Ned retch.

The gaoler handed him a small rushlight which he'd ignited from a torch.

"You can stay as long as that lasts," he said. "Give me a shout when it goes out. He's over there." He pointed into the blackness at the far corner of the cell, then shuffled out and locked the door.

Ned picked his way over prostrate bodies lying in their own vomit and worse. The gaol would be bad enough at the best of times, but today, after a fair, it was insufferable.

In the far corner, where the gaoler had indicated, Ned discovered what looked like the entrance to a tunnel, until he cast some light into it and found it to be a deep alcove off the main cell. Several sets of shackles hung from rings fixed to the dripping walls. One set was occupied by Jake, who, because of the shortness of the chain, sat on the floor with his hands up in front of him like a sleepwalker. Ned put the lamp carefully on the floor, smothered Jake in a huge embrace and launched into a mother's loud lament.

"O my son, my son! What have they done to you?"

Jake squirmed beneath him.

"Stow it, Ned," he hissed. "There ain't nobody goin' to notice you over here."

Ned stood back and squinted at Jake in the gloom. "'Od's teeth, Jake, but you've done it this time!" he whispered in his own voice. "They'll try you, send you away and I'll never see you no more, and that's the truth of it. You could hang for this if we can't spring you out o' here." He took the wig off and rubbed his head vigorously.

Jake used his shackles to haul himself to his feet, then winced as the hand irons cut into his wrists.

"Then do it quick. I don't want to stay in this hole no longer than what I have to. The gaoler'll let me slip if you give him enough, I know he will."

"I ain't got that sort o' money, Jake. He's not going to let you go for a few shillings, is he?"

"Then why'd you bother comin'?"

"Jake! You has to be the most ungratefulest cove I ever met. I should've let you rot till mornin' an' face the court."

"Wouldn't be the first time."

"But it might be the last! That's why I come. I have a plan, if you want to hear it."

Before he could explain, Ned heard a commotion outside. Raised voices, but not drunk. There was some kind of argument going on, and they were men of position by the sound of it. He clapped his wig back on as the door opened.

The gaoler came first, carrying a torch in one hand, an inkpot in the other, with quill and paper tucked under his arm. Then came the constable with what was obviously another prisoner. He half-dragged him across the floor and proceeded to shackle him to the wall beside Jake. Behind them was a well-dressed man holding a pomander to his nose, and another man, carrying a second torch and holding a frightened-looking youth by the shoulder.

From the tone of his voice, the man with the pomander sounded more than a little annoyed. "I hope you realize how privileged you are to be allowed access to the prisoner at this time."

The other man gave a snort of contempt. "Privilege be damned. You're the chief bailiff, it's your job to collect evidence, and I want to have a deposition of evidence made against this prisoner *now*."

"It could have waited till morning!" The chief bailiff was almost bursting with indignation. "Why the unseemly haste?"

"Unseemly? I do not consider it unseemly to wish to see justice done as quickly as possible. If we're to part his head from his shoulders, then let's get on with it. If we have evidence tonight, you can constitute the Gibbet Court tomorrow. Cloth stealing is rife in this town. Punishment must be seen to be both sure and swift if we are to deter those who would consider such action."

The man pushed the poor youth he was holding across the floor, heedless of whoever was in the way. He stumbled past Ned and Jake to the new prisoner, who was now hanging limply in his chains as if he were dead.

When they reached him, the accuser pushed the torch painfully close to the prisoner's face. It made him flinch and turn his head away.

"Is that him?" he asked the youth, thrusting him forward. "Is that the man?"

The boy gave a frightened look and whispered, "Yes, Mr. Womersley."

Womersley! Ned managed to turn his gasp into a cough. Suddenly he was all attention.

"Speak up, lad, tell the bailiff what you saw." Womersley gave him a dig in the back.

The boy glanced up, then took a deep breath and appeared to make up his mind.

"I saw that man," he said, pointing at the prisoner, "this afternoon at about two o' the clock, taking my master's cloth from the tenterframe in the field behind his house. He did not see me. I hid behind a tree and watched him carry the cloth away, bearing it on his back. Then I went and told my master." It was obvious that the young apprentice – if that's who he was – had been rehearsed in what to say.

The man smiled. "Thank you, Toby. That was what we needed to hear. You have the witness statement, and the stolen goods to produce in court. I think we have all the evidence we need to proceed to the gibbet. Did you get that down, Holroyd? Did you write it?"

Holroyd the bailiff, looking furious, handed the writing implements to the constable. Womersley stalked out of the gaol, thrusting the torch at Holroyd, and pulling the hapless Toby after him. The constable, the gaoler and the bailiff followed him out.

Ned slumped down on the bundle of filthy sacking that would have served as a bed, had Jake been able to lie down, and took his wig off again. The gaoler seemed to have forgotten the poor old woman amid all the excitement. The rushlight had gone out minutes ago. Jake was growing impatient.

"Well, what're you waitin' for?"

"I'm waitin' for the bailiff an' his retinue to be well clear o' the gaol before I act – it's not just your poxy skin I got to save now."

"What d'you mean?"

Ned didn't reply, but turned his attention to the new prisoner. Dark hair, deep-set eyes, firm chin – there was no doubting who he was. His shirt was filthy, torn and bloodstained. Ned could see red weals across his chest and shoulders. His nose was swollen and there was dried blood beneath it. A deep cut below one eye was still seeping. He had obviously put up stern resistance. His eyes were shut.

Ned put a hand to his shoulder. "You're Meg's father, ain't you?"

He stirred and half-opened his eyes. "Wha... what?"

"Meg – from Heptonstall."

The man came to life. "Meg? Where did you meet her? Isn't she at home?" His voice rose and he was becoming agitated.

Ned held up both hands. "Ssh. Don't make no fuss. Meg's all right. She's come lookin' for you, an' I'm helpin' her. She's back at the Cross. I'll take you there – as soon as I gets you out, that is."

"What about me?" Jake butted in.

"You too. I can as soon spring two as one."

A shuddering sob escaped from Meg's father's throat. "I can't believe you would do this for me, a complete stranger, putting yourself at risk."

"Look, I done time in gaol. I know what it's like. I don't know if you done what you're supposed to ha' done, but for every poor man in gaol there's a rich man walkin' free, with more crimes to his name than warts on a toad's back, an' if I can do somethin' to redress the balance, as you might say, then I'm happy to do it." He replaced his wig again. "Besides, your Meg deserves a bit o' help, so say no more. Just listen and I'll tell you how this great escape is goin' to happen."

Five minutes later, Ned began shouting and banging on the cell door, like someone terrified. He paused for a moment, until he heard the gaoler grumbling down the corridor, then began again.

"Orreet, orreet, no need to break the door down!" The gaoler obviously wasn't happy to have his peace disturbed again. After opening the door with some difficulty, he appeared with a torch in one hand and a bottle in the other. Scarcely had he set foot inside the cell before Ned clutched at his clothes.

"Thank goodness you've come!" he said, with all the appearance of relief, putting his face close to the gaoler's. "There's a presence in this place, an evil presence. The figure of a man appeared, his head and body parted asunder. His head was just a-bobbin' there, I tell you, foul obscenities coming out of its mouth." The gaoler pushed him away, and Ned stumbled and fell dramatically to the floor, pointing with a quivering finger to the far side of the cell. "There it is again!"

On cue, Meg's father and Jake started shaking and moaning too. The gaoler frowned and raised his torch, squinting in the direction of their gaze.

"There's nowt there. Are you all mad?"

"But can't you hear it, sir?" Ned looked at him in shocked surprise. The man took a step forward and put his head on one side. A low moan, growing louder and gradually higher in pitch, emanated from the vaulted ceiling. The gaoler took half a step backwards and raised the bottle to his lips, peering into the shadows.

There were words, now – hollow, ghostly words: "Death! Death but no death. Death and no resurrection. Death in life and life in death!" followed by a gurgling shriek somewhere between a scream and a laugh. The gaoler backed away, tottering, as drink and fear took hold of his legs. Ned could see sweat glistening on his forehead as he raised the torch in front of him in a protective gesture. A terrified cry burst involuntarily from his lips.

Ned scuttled forward on his knees now, weeping loudly.

"Don't say as you're afeared too, sir. We looked to you to save us!" He clasped the gaoler round the legs, causing him to topple over, sending bottle and torch crashing to the floor and plunging them all into darkness. Ned set up a fearful wail. "Who will save us now, sir? 'Tis some former prisoner bent on revenge, and he's a-comin' to get you!"

The gaoler was thrashing and flailing around in abject fear. Ned kept hold of him, shrieking and moaning, preventing him from gaining a foothold on the slippery floor. In the confusion, Ned's hand was moving gradually round the man's waist until his fingers closed on what the whole charade was about. The keys. He felt their coldness, and was just about to undo the loop they were attached to, when he became aware of a faint light shining through the door grille, and footsteps in the corridor. His heart sank. So near and yet so far. The person coming in was unlikely to be another drunken fool.

It was the constable, obviously making his final check of the evening, having seen Mr. Womersley and the bailiff on their way. Ned muttered a curse. His timing couldn't have been worse. The constable walked in.

"Gaoler? Everything all..." He stopped as he took in the scene revealed by his lantern. The gaoler was oblivious to the constable's arrival, rolling around on the floor in a fit of terror, bleeding from cuts he had sustained from the broken bottle that lay in pieces around him.

Ned pulled himself together and looked earnestly at the constable, trusting the poor light to preserve his disguise.

"Thank heaven your honour has arrived! There's a frightful apparition in the cell, come to haunt us!" He took hold of the constable's arm and pointed, quivering, to the corner of the cell, but there was no hope of fooling the constable. He looked depressingly sober. The escape attempt had failed.

12

News Of Father

Meg watched "Nan's sister" scuttle away across the yard. Ned hadn't said what he would do if he did find Mr. Sutcliffe, but he never seemed to be short of ideas. Waiting wasn't going to be easy; the dull feeling of not knowing had been replaced by a fretful impatience now that there was a lead to follow.

She wandered back to the hay pile, where Simon was looking at her figures.

"What's it like to be told you're a Maker?" he asked. "Do you feel any different?"

Meg thought for a moment. "Yes."

"Good or bad?"

She sat down beside him and held out her left hand.

"Can you do that?" she said, and brought her little finger down onto the palm without moving the others.

He moved his little finger down, but the others followed, no matter how much he tried to force them back.

"How do you do it?" he said, trying again.

"I don't know. It's just something I can do that other people can't – well, most people, anyway. I remember the first time I found out. I was by the village well and there were lots of people about, but none of them could do it. It was only a tiny thing, not important, but I felt quite excited. It made me feel different and special. Then next day I was walking down the street and two girls crossed over to avoid me, and I heard one say to the other, 'She's got funny fingers.' After that I was still glad I was different, but sometimes I wished I wasn't.

"Knowing I'm a Maker's like that, only bigger. I don't think I can hide it – not all the time. There must be other people like Ned, who sense it when they see my carvings. I wonder if Patience Sutcliffe does, only she can't understand and really thinks I'm tormenting her. Does it make *you* think differently about me?"

"Yes."

"Good or bad?"

Simon's brow gathered in a thoughtful frown. Without warning, he picked up a pile of hay and threw it at her. Meg was taken aback until she saw his mischievous grin.

"That's what I think of Makers and finger-wagglers," he said.

She wasn't going to let him get away with that! She picked up an armful and threw it back. "And that's what I think of lads who have visions!" More hay flew, until they were half-buried and looked like scarecrows come to life. Then they lay, laughing and breathless, looking up at the cobweb-ridden underside of the roof. It was good to know that, though Simon had just learned she was someone with special powers, he knew she was an ordinary lass as well.

The laughter over, Meg sat up, and couldn't prevent her eyes wandering to the edge of the hayloft, wanting to take a peep through the stables and into the yard.

Simon noticed. "Ned won't have got far yet."

"I know. But I can't help wondering."

"We need to find something to do." He rolled over and picked up Dilly-Lal. "How does she work? I'd like to see her dance." He handed her over.

Did Dilly-Lal want to dance? Of course she did. Any excuse.

"She'll dance," Meg said, taking the stick from

her bag and slotting it into Dilly-Lal's back. "I'll need a board."

There was a strip of wood hanging from a box in the corner. She pulled it off and put one end over the edge of the hayloft while she sat on the other, her legs dangling at either side. It had a good spring to it.

"Wait a minute," Simon said, "I'll fetch my fiddle." He disappeared through the door at the back of the loft that connected to the inn.

It was still noisy down below, though there weren't so many people around. One of the horses in the stalls was restless, plunging its head and whinnying. It had no bridle, but a groom caught its mane and tried to settle it, talking to it calmly.

Simon returned and sat beside her on the edge of the hayloft. Meg was intrigued by the fiddle. There was a fiddle maker in the village, but his work was rough and crude compared to this. She didn't know what kind of wood the body was made from, but great care had been taken to match up the grain, with a double lined border running round the edge.

But it was the scroll that caught Meg's attention most. It had been carved into the shape of a man's head, wearing an odd conical cap. The features of his face had been carefully and precisely done to give him a slightly smug expression. And Meg knew what kind of wood he was made of – it was hawthorn.

"I found this on a market stall in Derby," Simon said, noting her interest. "Scratched, dirty, no strings – and look at it now. There's a label inside." He held it up so she could peer through the f-hole. "The writing's Italian – so I've been told. I had to leave my old one behind when I fled from Dr. Challenor's. It was the one I learned on, sitting at my grandfather's knee and picking up his tunes.

"Right," he said, jumping up. "How about a jig?"

He started to play and Meg waited for Dilly-Lal to get a feel of the rhythm. She was keen to dance; her knees were trembling and one of her arms was circling round. Now she was ready! Meg pounded the board and set Dilly-Lal's feet clattering. The tune was one that Gaffer diddled to himself while he was working. He said it was called "Saddle the Pony" and he'd picked it up from Irish soldiers who passed through Heptonstall during the war.

Dilly-Lal loved it. The light from below cast a huge shadow on the underside of the loft roof. She was a giant, her arms and legs a blur of whirling movement, her head bobbing up and down. Simon was moving too, his body swaying forward and back as the bow went up and down, his left foot tapping out the beat and his eyes dancing as he played.

The tune came to an end and Simon finished with a final flourish, raising his arms aloft. To Meg's surprise, clapping and cheering broke out below. She'd had no idea they were being watched, but the grooms' faces were turned up towards her, and Nan was there too.

"Did y'ever see the like o' that?" she said to the grooms, and bustled over to the ladder. "There's me just come to see how they are, an' they're making merry wi' a dancing doll!"

There were a few other people too, and one of them made Simon draw in his breath and scramble back into the shadows. It was Big Hal the blacksmith.

"Hal says will you come down and perform for the company?" Nan said, and started to climb the ladder. "Says he didn't know what an excellent fellow you were when he caught you, and he 'opes you won't 'old it agin 'im – what 'appened afore."

Meg wasn't sure about it, and Nan must have caught a reluctant look on her face.

"An' don't worry," she said to her. "Hal'll look after thee. Ned told me what's up. We'll think about that in th' mornin', eh?"

"But I can't go down there," Simon said. "Not after what happened in the barroom."

Nan cackled and nearly lost her footing. "Don't you worry about that! There's nobbut locals left, an' we've no love o' constables at th' Cross. There's folks down there want to thank thee for amusing 'em so richly. So come down and be frolicsome!"

They were ushered through the stables and into the yard. The grooms had cleared a space in the middle, and set up a barrel with a board on top. One of them hoisted Meg up and an expectant hush fell on the crowd that had gathered round to watch. Dilly-Lal couldn't wait to start again. She wanted to show off, to have everybody admire her. Meg gave Simon a little nod. He drew his bow across the strings and began again.

It was a reel this time. Meg didn't know the tune, but the infectious rhythm caught her at once. Dilly-Lal danced as she had never danced before, and Meg felt quite dizzy. She noticed that Nan had taken her cap off and put it on the ground in front of the barrel. First a few pennies were thrown into it, then more, until the chink of money was yet another accompaniment to the dancing. The company started dancing too, grabbing the nearest person and whirling them round, until a circle formed round the barrel; forward and back it went, while one or two brave souls cavorted on their own in the middle, imitating Dilly-Lal's whirling arms and legs. Those who couldn't dance clapped and stamped and everyone was shouting and whooping, their faces shining in the flickering light.

Simon had played the tune twice through already and Meg's wrist was getting tired, but she went on until he had finished it a third time before lifting Dilly-Lal from the board. A great roar went up from the crowd. Were they cheering Meg, Simon or Dilly-Lal? There was no doubt what Dilly-Lal thought – her right arm was idling round, waving at the crowd. She was very pleased with herself.

Hal came up to them. He was even hotter and redder than before. He stretched his hand out in greeting. Meg saw Simon hesitate, no doubt remembering the crushing grip, then he thrust his hand firmly into Hal's, who shook it gently, and a stream of unintelligible, though obviously friendly, sounds came out of his tongueless mouth.

"He says he feels like dancing till dawn, an' would you like a bag o' nuts?" Nan said.

A bag was passed over. Simon helped himself and passed it to Meg, while Hal's grin almost split his face in two.

One or two people were shouting for more now, and the chant soon caught on. Should she bring Drum-a-Dum out too, Meg wondered?

Before she could decide, she saw Ned coming in through the archway. He pushed his way through the ring of spectators until he was standing next to Nan. Meg couldn't hear what they said, but Ned wasn't his usual jolly self, and now Nan looked gloomy too. Meg felt her heart hammering and exchanged glances with Simon. What had Ned found out?

He came to the barrel and jumped her down, lifting her by the elbows.

"We need to talk," he said. He was still dressed as an old woman, but he wasn't trying to sound like one or move like one. There were cries of protest from some of the company.

"I'll stay here," Simon said and struck up another tune. They were soon dancing again.

"Come on, we'd best get you back up to the loft." Ned's voice sounded gruff. His wig was slightly out of place and he hunched his shoulders as he led the way into the stables. He didn't even pause to give the ponies a pat as he usually did, but lumbered heavily up the ladder, making it shake every time he went up another rung.

There was something wrong. Meg waited until the ladder was still, then climbed up herself. Ned sat in the hay and took off his wig. He stretched his legs out, showing dirty, plum-coloured hose under his skirt.

"Sit ye down here, young Meg." He patted the hay beside him. "There's somethin' I has to tell you."

A cold feeling of dread began to well in Meg's stomach as she sat down.

"Now then... First things first. I've found your father."

Meg's heart leaped again, but there was no change in Ned's grave expression.

Ned took hold of her hands. "He's in gaol, I'm afraid."

"In gaol! But why?" Meg had been steeling herself for bad news, but not this. Father might have a quarrel with Mr. Sutcliffe, but she was sure he hadn't done anything against the law.

Ned went on as though he hadn't heard her. "An' if it hadn't been for the most wretched luck in the world, I'd've had him out by now."

Meg pulled her hands away, her mind whirling. "But what has he been accused of?" she asked, feeling angry, upset and disbelieving all at the same time. "When will they let him go?"

Ned looked at her strangely, as though he didn't want to tell her. "I...I don't know how long they'll keep him there. He's been accused of stealin' cloth from Womersley's tenterframe."

"Stealing cloth?" Meg was mystified. "Why would he want to do that? He has cloth of his own. He came to Halifax to sell it."

"I only knows what I heard in the gaol." Ned sighed. "A young lad called Toby dragged in by Womersley says he saw him carrying cloth on his back – if he's to be believed. But he said it there and then, in front o' the bailiff. He was so terrified I reckon he'd have said any mortal thing he was told."

"But that was Father's own cloth! He was taking it home again because prices were bad."

"It looks like they're goin' to make out it was Womersley's."

The scene at the inn came vividly back to Meg. She'd seen the looks Sutcliffe and Womersley had exchanged, and the money on the table. Was Sutcliffe paying Womersley to make up the theft and force Toby to tell those lies?

She looked at her wooden figures through a haze of tears. All Dilly-Lal's liveliness had drained away. Drum-a-Dum could show her exactly where Father was now, but that was no help. Bolly-Bolly had nothing to say.

Neither had Ned. He was hunched forward with his elbows on his knees and his chin cupped in his hands. He had tried to rescue Father from gaol, but he had failed.

13

THE BOOK

It was breakfast time at the Cross, and Meg was sitting with Simon and Ned at the corner table in the barroom, sharing a large quartern loaf and the remains of a ham shank. Apart from them, the barroom was empty. It felt strange and lifeless.

Everybody had been kind. Too kind. It almost felt as though Father was dead. Meg had managed to sleep a bit, though she kept waking up and worrying; about Father, about herself, even about Mother and Gaffer, wondering how they must be feeling. There was nothing they could do because they were in Heptonstall, and they had no idea where she or Father was. Maybe they thought she was still hiding around the village.

Even if they set off to search in the morning they wouldn't know where to go; Gaffer was old and lame, and Mother had Robert to look after. Meg had set off to find Father, expecting him to protect her, but now the tables were turned. It was up to her to get him free, despite the danger to herself. At least she knew where he was.

In the middle of the night she'd talked to Bolly-Bolly. He'd been grumpy at being woken up, and didn't want to cooperate, but Meg had made him. She could do that when it really mattered. She wanted to know if he could see what was going to happen to Father. He tried, but he couldn't. Everything was misty-swirly. What did Meg expect? He wasn't a fortune teller or a soothsayer. And he thought she was silly for being so sad. Oddly enough, she'd felt better after that, and went back to sleep quite quickly.

Simon was reading a letter. Meg wondered whether that was something Dr. Challenor had taught him to do, or whether it was something he had "picked up", like playing the fiddle. He looked up when he'd finished.

"You can read it if you like," he said when he'd finished, handing it to Ned.

Ned shook his head. "You'd best read it to me; the old eyes ain't what they was. Then Meg can hear it too – if you don't mind, that is."

"Why should I mind? We're friends." He shook the letter and took up a pose. "To Master Simon Jolly, if perchance he should wonder at my absence." Meg had wondered who the letter was from, but there was no doubt now; Simon had caught Giles Gillyflower to the life.

"Sir, though I treated you as mine own son, you have not been kind to me. As my apprentice and trusted assistant, I looked to have had more diligence in the performing of your duties, and more gratitude for the position I generously bestowed upon you. And now you bring shame upon the good name of Dr. Bonum by engaging in such doubtful activities as caused you to make an unseemly commotion in the inn, and almost to be arrested! I proceed to Pendle alone, and hereby relieve you of all formal and informal obligations, and consider myself likewise relieved. GG."

Meg hadn't seen much of "Dr. Bonum", but enough to know that this was exactly the sort of letter he would write. Ned laughed and shook his head. "Ain't that just like old Giles. Touchy, you see. Imagines hisself hard done by and gets on his high horse. Though I reckon your dismissal has more to do with interruptin' him in bed than with any shortcomings of your own! But it's an ill wind... as they say. There's you without a master and me without an assistant. What's more natural than we team up together, eh? I ain't known you long, but you get to be a shrewd judge o' character when you're travellin', an' I reckons we'd rub along well, you an' me."

"But what about Jake?" Simon asked. "Don't you think he'll go free?"

Ned rocked his stool back and let out a long breath. "Maybe, maybe not. But I suspect it's goin' to take time. If they sends him to York, which like as not they will do, it could be weeks before he comes to trial. I could plead his case – as I've done times before – but whether he hangs or goes free could depend on what the judge has for lunch. Pickled herrin' or lampreys might be enough to sign Jake's death warrant. I won't deny as he has a habit o' wormin' his way out o' custody in ways what leave me baffled, but I reckon I've been fair with him, stuck to him through thick an' thin – an' it's mostly been thin. Meanwhile, I has a livin' to make. And so do you. Jake ain't got no grounds to complain if I ditch him."

"But why did you stick with him till now?" Meg had wondered this right from the start.

Ned looked a bit shamefaced. "It ain't somethin' I'm proud of, but, like Simon says, we're friends. Events have kind o' thrown us together, ain't they? There's no reason why you shouldn't know.

"I thought he was mine – my son, that is."

Meg was amazed at Ned's revelation. It would be hard to imagine two individuals who were more different, both physically and temperamentally. She thought for a moment that Ned might be having a joke, but his face was unusually serious.

"He might ha' been. I knew his mother, y'see. We was friends, then more than friends for a while, but she turned out to be a bit of a flirt-gill, an' I...well, I wasn't much better. We drifted apart after a few months. Then, a few years ago, she turns up at a fair in Abingdon where I was performin', with this scrawny youth. 'He's yours,' she says. 'I've looked after him since he was born – now it's your turn.' So I took him on. But I don't seem to ha' done him much good."

"You said you *thought* he was your son." Meg was puzzled by how you could think but not be sure. "Does that mean he isn't?"

"So I've been told. His mother died a few months ago, an' confessed on her deathbed as I *wasn't* his father. I just found out last week in Pontefract. She told her confessor she wanted me to know, but as to who the real father was, she swore him to secrecy.

"Even so, I'm reluctant to cast him off. If I thought I could influence him for the better... But you see how he is. We've come to the partin' o' the ways. So how about it, Simon? Are you goin' to throw in your lot with old Ned?"

Simon looked as though he was still trying to get over the surprise of losing one position and being offered another in a matter of minutes.

"But...but I don't know how to work the puppets."

"You can learn. It ain't that difficult."

"And I've never so much as built a snowman – I couldn't make anything."

"I've got a fair old stock – should keep us going for a while. I'll make what we needs. I can't put the life in 'em, but maybe that's no bad thing. When I looks at Jake's work sometimes it gives me a shudderin' fit."

"Well, if you're sure..." He looked at Meg to see what she thought. She smiled and nodded, glad that at least her friends had something to celebrate.

Simon and Ned shook hands, while Nan, who had been hovering nearby, came to add her congratulations.

The silence that followed was a long one and Meg knew why. They were feeling happy and she wasn't. None of them had any idea what to do about her father. Ned coughed, but it sounded false and hollow in the empty room.

"I think..."

"Maybe..."

Both Ned and Nan started to talk at once, but stopped. It was Simon who made the first suggestion.

"Should we go to the chief justice?" Nobody said no straight away, so he went on. "We can tell him that Meg's father is innocent," he said to Ned. "If he's been falsely accused, then other people should be arrested, not him. I suppose it depends whether the justice is a fair-minded man or not."

Ned sighed and shook his head. "If the justice ain't a fair-minded man, he ain't goin' to be on our side, is he? An' if he *is* a fair-minded man, he's goin' to listen to both sides. I don't see how we can stop this from comin' to court. A deposition of evidence has been made against John Lumb by an eyewitness, an' the bailiff's got it – all legal and proper. An' they've got the stolen goods to produce in court. We ain't got no evidence o' nothin'."

That wasn't quite true, Meg suddenly realized.

"That cloth wasn't stolen, it was Father's own." She was full of excitement now. "If they put it with some other pieces I could pick it out, even if it was the same colour. That would prove it was his and not Mr. Womersley's, wouldn't it?"

She'd expected everybody to be as delighted as she was, but Ned remained grave. "It would, if it was his cloth what's produced in court, but there ain't much chance o' that. They'll swap it. It'll be Womersley's cloth they show. We can't risk bringin' you out o' hidin' for that."

Meg felt as though someone had thrown a bucket of cold water in her face. What Ned said sounded sadly true. Even good ideas didn't always work.

"I don't think innocent or guilty 'as a lot to do wi' it," Nan said. "The last one they gibbeted were innocent."

Ned jumped up and clapped his hand over her mouth, but it was too late. He looked round at Meg in despair. "I'm sorry. We was trying to keep the worst from you."

They were trying to be kind again, but there was no child in Halifax or the whole of the Calder valley who didn't know about the gibbet. Young children were warned that if they weren't good the gibbet man would take them away and chop their heads off. Meg had always known that wasn't true, but she knew what it *was* used for. And she'd seen Ned's motion.

Nan coughed and gasped as she was released and gave Ned a scornful look. "I was just going to say as how that's a *good* sign. If they got it wrong last time, they'll make sure they don't make the same mistake again, won't they? If they've any doubts at all, they'll release 'im. There's plenty in Halifax thinks the gibbet should be done away with.

"I'll never forget when Joseph Shackleton were done. When th' blade come down there were silence. No cheering. Everybody knew as he were innocent. A kinder man never lived. An' when his head fell off into th' basket, a ray o' sunlight struck through a rent in th' clouds an' lit it up. Then a halo formed over it, and through the 'alo his mortal soul rose up th' shaft of sunlight unto 'eaven. Saw it wi' me own eyes, I did.

"I think we should go and mek a fuss. Shout his innocence loud. There's others'll join us. Maybe we can influence th' jurors. An' I'll tell the court I seen 'im with 'is own piece."

"Can't do no harm, can it?" Ned said. He got to his feet, brushing crumbs from his shirt onto the table. "While there's life there's hope. Let's be goin'."

Meg jumped up, but Ned held up his hand. "You're in danger too, don't forget. There's folks lookin' for you, an' I reckon you're safer here than outside. Simon'll stay with you."

She supposed Ned was right, but she didn't want to stop behind. There must be *something* she could do. It seemed wrong that he and Nan were the ones who were going to try and help while she was stuck in the hayloft.

Meg lined her figures up on the hayloft floor in front of her, but they weren't able to make her feel any better. Dilly-Lal sat with her legs stuck out and her arms by her side, not a spark of rhythm in her. Drum-a-Dum's string had become tangled round his neck and arms but he didn't care. And Bolly-Bolly wanted to know why she had allowed Ned to persuade her to stay up here when her father was about to be condemned to death. Possibly. That wasn't what she wanted to hear, so she put him back in the bag.

It was impossible not to become more and more anxious.

Simon found it easier to stay calm. He was lolling back on the hay looking at a book. Meg even wondered if he was reading it. But, although his eyes were fixed on the page, his lips weren't moving – and how could you know what the words were if you didn't say them?

"Are you reading?" she asked.

Simon looked up. "Yes."

"Is it hard?'"

Simon put his book down and sat up. "I've never thought about it."

"I know some reading," Meg said, moving nearer to Simon's pile of hay. "M.A.R.T.H.A. That's Martha. It's on a gravestone. Can I have a look?" She held her hands out and Simon passed the book over.

Meg had never held a book before, or seen one close to. The vicar read from a big book in church, but this was different. You could hold it in your own hands. She ran her fingers over the cover. It was made of leather, scuffed and worn with a lot of handling. She laid the book on her lap and looked inside. The pages were thick and carefully stitched together. They felt slightly rough when she rubbed one between her thumb and finger. If you looked closely you could see the tiny pieces of straw or wood that it was made of.

Father had pieces of paper at home, but they were thinner than this – receipts, he called them – and they were important, though he couldn't read what was on them any more than she could. They were given to him at the market when he sold his weaving. If there was any dispute afterwards, he could produce his receipt and prove what he'd sold, when he'd sold it, who he'd sold it to and for how much.

When the book was opened out there were pictures of flowers and other plants on one side, with words opposite. So many words, so small and close together. Not like the names on a gravestone. How could you ever know what they all said?

Meg liked the pictures. She wondered who had drawn and coloured them all as she turned through the pages. She had no idea there were so many different plants. Most of these she'd never seen before and she thought she was good at flower names. A few of the pages had flowers dried and pressed between them. Some were like the flowers in the hay – all brown and fragile, ready to crumble away to nothing – which might have been why there weren't more – but others had kept their colour, and looked almost as fresh as the flowers she'd seen in the graveyard yesterday.

Yesterday? Was it really only yesterday? It didn't take long for your whole life to turn upside down.

"It's not a printed book," Simon said. "Dr.

Challenor wrote it and made it. Even the paper and the stitching. And the cover."

Meg looked at the outside again. The words had been tooled into the leather. She ran her little finger round the letters. This was more like a gravestone.

"What's it called?" she asked.

"*Dr. Challenor's Complete Herbal*. He put everything he knows about plants and healing into it." Simon sat beside her and turned the pages, stopping at one. "Look, here's one you'll know."

It was coltsfoot; she recognized the big flat leaf and yellow flower.

Simon pointed to the writing with his finger. "First he describes it, then he tells you where you can find it, when it flowers, and then what it's good for. 'The fresh leaves, or juice, or syrup thereof, is good for a hot, dry cough, or wheezing, and shortness of breath.'"

Meg was fascinated. Rows and rows of neat, orderly words that told you all about it. Not like the writing on the receipts, which was big and scratchy. You could sometimes see where ink had spurted from the quill and made a little line of blots. There was nothing like that on Dr. Challenor's page. He must have taken great care.

The picture was even more delicately done. The outline of the coltsfoot leaf must have been made with a brush; it was finer and softer than the writing and there were tiny feathery curls where the brush had been lifted off. The space inside the outline had been coloured green and there were even faint lines showing veins, and tiny spots and blemishes like you would find on a real leaf. And each of the dozens of thin, feathery petals of the flower had been done with a single, separate stroke. It looked as though it had just burst into bloom.

Meg was in awe of *Dr. Challenor's Complete Herbal.* All Dr. Challenor's knowledge and understanding of plants and their uses was there in those closely written pages, and anyone who could read could know it too, without ever seeing or hearing Dr. Challenor. Or even knowing who he was. It was magic.

But there was another kind of magic there, and it had to do with the making. Dr. Challenor had made the book with his own hands. He had made the paper and formed the pages. Maybe he had even skinned the beast the leather had come from and cured it himself; had made his own ink and paints from pigments he had ground. Then he had made the writing with his pen and the pictures with his brush.

Like her own carving, he had put the life in it. Meg could sense that there was life in the book, in the fabric of its paper and the substance of its ink. Whatever other skills he had, Dr. Challenor was a Maker, like she was, but one of great wisdom and experience. The magic in the book was deep and powerful.

"It's not the sort of thing you give away," she said, closing it and handing it back to Simon. "Why have you got it?"

"He gave it to me when he had to leave in a hurry. I expect he'll want it back one day – if he can find me. If he isn't dead or in prison."

"Why should you think he might be?"

"He had enemies, and they were closing in on him. He feared arrest – I don't know the exact reason – that's why he had to get away. I was in the back of the shop one day, making up remedies, when he came bursting in. He said he was 'undone', and told me to run, or they might take me too. Then he started pulling papers from drawers and cupboards and feeding them into the little brazier we had on the hearth. 'Why don't you run too?' I said, but he ignored me. Then he took the book off the shelf where it always sat so it was handy, and pushed it into my hands. I'll never forget what he said then: 'Take this and go. Keep up your studies and you'll be an apothecary – and a visionary – one day.' But I don't know how I can be a visionary if I don't know what my visions are about. I need him to teach me."

The idea of Simon as a visionary made Meg smile. The only ones she had ever seen were in the stained glass windows in Heptonstall church, before the Puritans succeeded in having them removed. Those visionaries had been holy men with halos and they only saw saints and angels. Not at all like Simon.

"So how did you meet Giles?" she asked.

"I'd seen his stall at Bartholomew Fair, so I went down there and asked him if he wanted any help – I thought he might be able to teach me something. All he's taught me is how to make bogus claims for his so-called cures. All you need to sell them are a lot of coloured bottles and a silver tongue. Dr. Challenor wasn't like that. He wouldn't sell anything if he didn't think it would do some good."

Meg had always thought that masters and apprentices didn't like each other, but Simon cared about his master, and his master cared about him and wanted him to learn, or he wouldn't have given him the book. Not like Giles Gillyflower. He'd never been Simon's real master. And she didn't think Ned would be either – he could teach Simon about puppets, but not about physic, or visions, though they would get on well enough.

Simon stood up. "Ned asked me to take the ponies down to the smithy," he said. "I won't be long."

Meg made a decision, and got to her feet. "I'm coming too."

"But Ned said—"

"I know what Ned said, but I'd rather be outside with you than here on my own."

"But it may not be safe."

"Who knows? I may not be safe up here. It *feels* safer when there are two of us." She grabbed his hand and pulled him to the ladder.

14

DISCOVERED

As they led the ponies from the stable, it was strange to see everybody going about their business as if nothing unusual was happening. There was a little market going on in the inn yard. Dead game – pheasant, partridge, hare – hung from iron hooks on the wall beside the stable door, and a woman was buying hens. They were crammed into a basket with the lid shut down. There were windows in the side of the basket, and some of the hens had pushed their heads out, ruffling their neck feathers on the rough wickerwork. Meg wondered if there were any more in the basket that couldn't push their heads out. It must be like being in a crowded prison. That thought made her want to weep again. She tugged at the pony's leading rein and hurried after Simon, who was disappearing through the gateway.

The street was a mess. Meg watched a butcher throw out a bucketful of offal to join the slops from upstairs windows and rubbish from yesterday's fair. A pack of stray dogs pounced on it, snapping and snarling at each other as they pulled at gory pieces of lungs and guts. It was easy to see why everybody seemed to be wearing clogs or pattens. Meg only wore clogs in the winter. Father used to make them, but now she did.

Father, Father, Father. She couldn't prevent her thoughts going back to him all the time.

She looked up the street. The view was dominated by the stark form of the gibbet. People walked past it without even a glance. Some were sitting on the stone platform that formed its base. Children ran round it, swinging on the framework.

They walked on until they reached the smithy. A lad appeared – Hal's apprentice, presumably – and asked them to tether the ponies on a patch of grass.

"I'm Tom," he said. "Hal will shoe 'em soon," and disappeared back inside. They secured the ponies to a couple of stakes and made their way back along the street.

The gibbet was much bigger than Meg had

imagined. The stone platform alone was above her head, with steps leading up to it. She leaned her head back and looked to the top of the frame. With clouds scudding above, it looked as if it was toppling over.

"I'm going to have a closer look," she said.

"Are you sure?" Simon sounded surprised. She was shocked herself, but she had an odd compulsion to go right up to it – like looking your enemy in the eye. She walked up the steps with Simon behind her. He seemed to be more uncomfortable than she was.

On the platform, at the foot of the wooden framework, Meg felt strangely calm. There were two thick uprights set into the stonework, and a massive wooden block between them which held the blade. Meg could see how it worked. There were grooves on the insides of the uprights so that the block could travel up and down. There was no blade in it just now, and it was firmly wedged at the bottom.

The uprights, braced at the sides and back to keep them firm, were nearly as thick as the roof beams in the hayloft at the Cross. People had scratched and carved things on them – faces, names, initials twined together. What made lovers want to carve their names on a gibbet? Maybe it was like wishing for bad luck so the opposite would happen.

There was some writing up one side. Meg turned to ask Simon what it was, but he read it aloud before she could speak.

"Jennet I love thee. Be mine till my nekke be severd. Jack."

Meg wondered what had happened to Jack. Did he really have his head chopped off, or was it a sort of joke? Simon was looking at the bottom of the frame, below the carvings. A plant with small yellow flowers grew from a crack between two platform stones and crept round the bottom of the gibbet. He bent down and picked a length of stem with several flowers and leaves on it and handed it to her.

"Cinquefoil," he said. "Dr. Challenor's herbal says it's for good luck and justice. Protection and defence, too."

Meg wished she had a book to press it in. She popped it in her bag. As she did so, her fingers brushed the cloth her little shut-knife was wrapped in. Almost without her willing them, they closed in on it and took it out.

There were narrow splits in the grain of the gibbet frame when you looked closely at the wood. Meg unwrapped her knife and pushed the point in at an angle, close to one of the splits and drew it down the grain. A thin sliver came off, even though the wood was hard. The surface was weathered and greyish, but inside the wood was a warm, dark brown, like old furniture.

Further up was a knot where a branch had been and the grain spread round it. Meg followed it round with her knife. She did the same at the other side, and she saw what it was she was carving. It was a tree with the sun caught in its branches.

There was a tree in the churchyard that she could see from the window at home. At this time of year, when the sun set, it went down right behind the tree. Blood-red sometimes. As if the tree were bleeding.

At that point the knife took over. It didn't take long to finish; a few more vertical cuts for the trunk, and some cross-grain cuts for the branches, and there it was. She had never etched an image like this before, but, like the dolls she made, it had come from the *influence* within her. The power of the Maker.

She inscribed a leaf shape above the tree – an oak leaf – and the link became clear to her. The gibbet was made of oak wood; dead, weather-beaten, hardened with age, and she had carved on it the representation of a live oak, one that grew and quickened, shedding its leaves in autumn and putting forth new buds in spring. A symbol of hope. She shut and wrapped her knife carefully and put it away.

Only then did Meg notice what had happened to Simon. She had been working so intently that everything else had been blotted out. He was crumpled up at the bottom of the gibbet. One look at his face and she knew instantly what had happened – he had fallen into another trance. He must have felt it coming on, and that was why he hadn't wanted to come right up to the gibbet. He had given her a cinquefoil – protection and defence – but he should have kept it for himself.

She glanced around, almost expecting to see Jake lurking in the shadow of the platform, but he was in gaol. The model gibbet, full of Jake's own evil thoughts had been the trigger for Simon's last vision, but this was the real thing. Had similar thoughts gone into its making? Those who had sawed and chopped the wood would have known what its purpose would be.

Should she try and get help or just wait until Simon came round again? Meg felt panic rising. She was worried about Simon, even though she had seen him collapse like this before, and she was worried about herself, about drawing attention to herself if she made a fuss. If only Ned was here! She looked around for a sympathetic face, but everyone was going about their own affairs. A few people spared Simon a glance, and she heard one tut-tut and mutter, "Drunk."

And then she saw two faces that put all other thoughts out of her mind. She felt the blood drain from her face, and fear stab at her stomach. They weren't friendly faces, but ones she dreaded. Mr. Sutcliffe and the Reverend Nathaniel Eastwood were talking to each other in the street.

They hadn't seen her, but they were coming towards the gibbet, and if either were to glance up now he couldn't miss her. Meg ran to the back edge of the gibbet platform and jumped off. It was a longer drop than she expected, but she kept her feet. Her instinct was to run down towards the Hebble brook, but if she did that she would soon be seen – there was nothing to hide her. Crouching on hands and knees, she pushed herself as close to the wall as possible, her heart pounding, gasping for breath as though she'd run all the way down the street.

At first she could just hear a babble of voices from the other side of the platform. Then the two voices of Sutcliffe and Eastwood detached themselves from the rest. It was hard to hear what they were saying, but they must have climbed up the steps and now be standing somewhere above her.

A fringe of grass grew along the back edge of the platform, unlike at the front, where people going up and down the street found a convenient resting place. Meg stood up, gripped the top stones with her fingers, and cautiously pulled herself on tiptoe. She could just see the men through the grass stems. They had their backs to her and were deep in conversation, taking no heed of Simon slumped at their feet. Maybe they too thought he was drunk. They didn't know who he was, of course.

Without warning, Eastwood turned round, and for a moment Meg was convinced he had seen her, even though she bobbed down immediately. But he hadn't. He was still talking to Sutcliffe and she could hear their voices clearly.

"But why didn't you tell me about the cloth-stealing yesterday?"

"Because, Reverend, it was none of your business." Sutcliffe was scathing. "It still isn't. I told you as much as you needed to know. I don't make a habit of discussing my affairs with others. So far as I'm concerned, the less folks know about them the better. That's always served me well. But now Lumb's been charged and faces the Gibbet Court you're bound to know."

"Do you mind telling me what happened?"

There was a pause before Sutcliffe replied. "Yes, I do. But it'll be common knowledge soon enough, so you may as well hear it from me. At least you'll get the right tale.

"Early yesterday afternoon, John Lumb was on his way back to Heptonstall, having sold his piece. The way goes past Edgar Womersley's place, and there was cloth drying on the tenterframes beside the track. Lumb had the effrontery to help himself, to unhook a piece and make off with it. Fortunately, the apprentice saw him, and two of Womersley's men were soon in pursuit. He gave them the slip, as you know, but they found him in the church at the finish up. They had to drag him off his knees. What d'you think o' that?"

The minister didn't say what he thought. When he spoke again, his words were slow and deliberate. "I understand your concerns over John Lumb and the threat he poses to your business. It would no doubt give you a great deal of satisfaction if he were to pay the ultimate penalty for stealing Edgar Womersley's cloth, but it is out of your hands now. Why are you waiting around idly for news of him instead of moving heaven and earth to find his daughter? I have been making enquiries since first light, but it's *your* daughter's life that's at stake, surely—"

"Enough!"

"But Isaac, you haven't seen Patience since early yesterday morning. If you had seen what I—"

"I said enough!" Sutcliffe's voice was harsh with anger. "She is being looked after by her mother and her fate is in the hands of God. Meg Lumb will turn up. I don't intend to run myself ragged looking for her. You should heed your own words. Prayer and fasting, you say, are our only defence against such wickedness. So why aren't you praying – or fasting? I noticed you enjoyed a good breakfast."

"I pray, Isaac. God knows I pray. But there is a time for action. My concern is not for Patience alone. I fear that if Meg Lumb is not caught, questioned and escorted back to Heptonstall immediately, then others may be affected. That is the urgency. It is but rarely that the malice of a witch lights upon one alone."

"And you fear for your own family." There was contempt in Sutcliffe's voice.

"That I admit. There is surely no shame in it."

Meg was trembling. Sutcliffe and the minister were

only feet away, and if they were to see her... She didn't let her mind finish that thought.

Their voices had gone quieter. They must have turned round. Meg risked another peep. They had their backs to her again. Sutcliffe had his hands grasped behind him, while Eastwood stood with his head bowed. She could just hear what Sutcliffe was saying.

"The Gibbet Court will very soon meet in closed session. I shall wait outside for their decision on the fate of John Lumb. I must see this affair to a conclusion." He swung round again and Meg ducked down. "After that I'll ride to Heptonstall. But I hope to have cause to return here tomorrow for Lumb's execution. It would be good to see this device put to use."

The minister didn't reply, and Meg heard feet scraping directly above her. She could see Eastwood standing on the edge of the platform looking into the distance. She held her breath and tried to squeeze even closer to the wall. Then, to her horror, he glanced down. Meg was staring straight into his eyes.

First surprise, then triumph lit up the minister's gaunt features.

"If you ever doubt the power of prayer, Isaac, just look down here," he said.

Sutcliffe's face appeared. His astonishment did nothing to dispel the cruel glint that never left his eyes.

The minister raised his hands to the heavens. "Wonderful are the ways of the Lord. He hath delivered the enemy into our hands."

Meg felt transfixed like a coney in a lamper's beam, unable to move, think, feel. She cowered under their gaze, as if trying to shrink into herself to the point where she became invisible. In a few moments they would lay their rough hands on her and drag her away. Her struggle was at an end; whatever happened to her – and Father – now would depend on other people.

Then, from what seemed like another world, she heard cries of alarm. Her eyes instinctively looked up and what she saw seemed to come from another world too. Sutcliffe and Eastwood were no longer standing on the gibbet platform, they were in mid-air. In a tangle of arms and legs they shot over her and crashed to the ground. The face that had looked at her so cruelly was now open-mouthed and contorted in pain.

"Meg! Meg!"

Someone was calling her. She looked up to the platform again, and there was Simon holding a hand down to her. Her body reacted before her mind had taken in the situation. She grabbed Simon's hand and braced her feet against the stonework as he hauled her up to the top.

"What did you do?" she asked, as they ran to the front of the platform and down the steps into the busy street.

"Pushed them off. I don't think anyone saw me. We'd better get back to the hayloft quickly – we haven't got long."

"I don't think we'll be safe there, Simon. We need somewhere else to hide."

Simon looked round, as though a hiding place might suddenly appear from nowhere.

"Let's go back to the smithy. We can think what to do when we get there."

They set off running, but Simon suddenly slowed in hesitation.

"What is it?"

"My fiddle – and the Herbal. I don't want to leave them at the Cross. You go on – I'll see you at the smithy in a minute."

"But Simon, you'll..."

It was too late. He'd already gone the other way and was lost in the crowd. Meg scampered up the street. She glanced back once. The two men were still on the ground, but there was someone else there now, bending over them – another man, though she couldn't tell what he looked like. She wondered how badly hurt Sutcliffe and Eastwood were. Maybe they had broken legs and wouldn't be able to come after her any more. But they would tell others. Now that she had been seen and recognized – and possibly Simon too – they would alert the whole town.

15

SHADOW ON THE HILLSIDE

By the time she reached the smithy, Meg was hot and out of breath. A shower of sparks greeted her, and a blast of hot air from the furnace. Big Hal was working on a red-hot horseshoe held to the anvil by Tom with a long pair of tongs. Hal paused and mumbled something to her.

"He says to tell you the ponies aren't ready yet," Tom translated.

"That's not what I've come for," Meg gasped, holding her side. "Something's happened. We need to hide. Simon'll be here soon."

Hal nodded his understanding and motioned her in, where she slipped into the shadows at the back of the smithy. Tom plunged the newly made horseshoe into a trough of water, causing it to sizzle and steam.

He took it out and slotted it onto a pole with a row of others.

Before she'd got her breath back, Simon appeared in the entrance with a bag slung over his shoulder, his fiddle bow sticking out of the top. Hal's face split into a huge grin and he enfolded Simon in a bear hug, followed by a stream of sound.

"He says he's right pleased to see you," Tom said. "And didn't you have the most capersome time last night. He hasn't enjoyed himself so much since the king lost his head."

Simon struggled free from Hal's embrace and moved further in to join Meg. "I think we need to get out of town." Meg had never seen him look so worried. "There's a big stir out there already."

Hal had stopped work, and was leaning against his anvil, listening.

"Two men are searching for Meg," Simon explained to him. "And they mustn't catch her. They may be after me too. We need to go where they won't find us."

Hal laughed; a strange squeak in his tongueless mouth, and made a large fist. It was clear what he would do to anyone who might threaten them. Then he started talking again.

"He says you should go to his old mother's house at Jowler," Tom said. "Tell her Hal's sent you and she'll look after you like you were her own son and daughter. We'll tell Ned where you've gone."

When they had all the details, Simon grabbed Meg's hand, but she pulled it away. "What about Father?" It felt as if she was running away and leaving him to his fate.

"It'll just make matters worse if you get caught."

Simon was right. It wouldn't help Father if she was captured too, and that was far more likely if she stayed in town now. She would have to rely on Ned and Nan to do their best.

Meg leaned against a drystone wall, catching her breath and cooling down after the toil up the hillside. They were well away from the town now, and agreed to rest for a few minutes before tackling the rest of the journey. They must be more than halfway to Hal's mother's cottage, and Meg was beginning to feel less of the suppressed panic that had been with her since Simon had slumped to the ground.

"Did you have another vision of the gibbet?" She'd been wondering, but hadn't felt like asking until now.

"No." Simon's eyes were searching the way they

had come for any signs of pursuit. "I wasn't so involved in this one – just watching. A stag was being chased by a pack of hounds."

"Sounds like us."

Simon turned to her with a puzzled expression. "It was strange at the end. The stag was almost at its last gasp, with the hounds ready to pounce, when they came to a stream. The stag waded through it and collapsed on the ground, but the hounds couldn't follow. They stood on the bank, baying in frustration. No idea what it means." He climbed the wall and peered over the other side. "There's no one in sight. Let's go."

Meg put her feet in the gaps between the stones, and pulled herself to the top as Simon jumped down. She could see where they were heading now. A cart track ran beside the wall, along a ridge between two valleys. They had just climbed out of one, and now they had to go down into the next. Hal had told them to look out for a landmark – an outcrop of rock shaped like a cat, with an inn below it. She could see the cat, a little way up the far side of the valley. It was asleep, with its head on its paws and its tail curled round, the swell of the hillside like a quilt about it. Meg jumped down beside Simon and they ran across the track.

A narrow path led them to a river, and a little way downstream Meg could see a wooded clough, which was where Hal's mother lived. They crossed a humpbacked bridge to the inn Hal had mentioned. It was called The Cat i' th' Well. It wasn't a traveller's inn – no stabling, not even a trough to water any passing horses. The door was shut and there was no sign of the life and bustle you would expect. A single thin dog appeared and gave them a pathetic look – it didn't even bark.

They turned their backs on it and took the path towards the clough. It would have been difficult to follow if it weren't for the wall – the only other indication of its route a slight flattening of the grass. Meg wondered if anyone other than Hal's mother ever used it.

It was quiet – too quiet; no birdsong, no wind to rustle the trees and grass. Even the sound of the water was muffled. It was so quiet she could hear the faint rushing in her ears that Gaffer called "the sound of nothing". Everything seemed to be holding its breath.

Then something caught her attention. Whether she saw it first or sensed it, she wasn't sure, but there was movement in a thin line of trees that straggled out from denser woods at the head of the clough. She stared up the hillside and pointed. There was little undergrowth to screen anything from view, but it was difficult to see clearly in the pattern of light and shade beneath the trees.

"I expect it's a sheep," Simon said.

Meg shook her head.

"A fox, then?"

"It didn't move like that," she said, and there was a tremor in her voice. "It...it was more like a person doubled over."

She peered harder at the trees, but she couldn't see it now. It might have broken cover and be out in the open, but hidden from them by the wall. She climbed up until she could see over the top, gripping the capping stones tightly.

"I can't see anything," she said. "I think it's gone lower down into the shelter of the wood."

"Does it matter?"

Was Simon just trying to dismiss it, or did he really want to know; trusting her judgement? She wasn't sure. She removed one foot from its hold, to climb down.

One moment she was clinging to the wall, her foot swinging wildly, and the next she was lying on her back in the long grass at the bottom, with Simon bending anxiously over her. She wasn't hurt, but how had she come to fall? She'd felt a push – she was sure of it. Not a hard push, but enough to make her lose her balance.

"Are you all right?" Simon asked.

She picked herself up and tried to laugh it off, but she felt tense and anxious and, by the look in his eyes, it was affecting Simon too. He didn't say anything, but set off again, rather too quickly, along the path.

There was one other thing that disturbed her: Bolly-Bolly had jumped inside his bag. He wasn't just rattled around by her fall, he had definitely jumped. Whatever it was out there, he didn't like it.

Then came the sound. Somewhere ahead of them, but impossible to pinpoint. It was difficult to describe – part shriek, part bark; hard to tell whether it was human or animal, but it made Meg go cold. What kind of creature would make a sound like that? Then it came again – once, twice more.

Meg's mind went back to Gaffer's story about the Skriker – the creature that told you when death was coming. Was that what she had seen skulking among that line of sycamores? If it was the Skriker, why had it come? Was it telling her that her father was going to die?

She felt sick and tears pricked her eyes again. What were they doing out here when her father was in peril of his life in Halifax? She was having second thoughts about this running away; it seemed wrong. She had been panicked into thinking it was the best thing to do in the face of her own peril – and Simon's. Now, she wasn't so certain. She had friends in Halifax who would hide her, defend her if needs be. Halifax was a big place and there were so many people there; Sutcliffe and Eastwood couldn't search everywhere. And maybe, just maybe, there was something she herself could do to help.

"Simon!" she said, stopping on the path.

He turned.

"I think I should go back."

"What?"

She waited until he came close to her, his eyes wide with surprise. "I could hide in town. There might be something more I could do to help Father. I don't expect you to come."

"But your father might even be free by now, who knows?"

"You don't really believe that, do you?"

Simon hesitated and his face clouded. "I don't know. But I still think we should go to Hal's mother's

– it's not far now, and you'll be out of harm's way there. It would be risky to go back – one more thing for Ned and the others to worry about."

That sounded true, but Meg was only partly convinced. She ought to be where Father was, making sure that everything possible was being done to save him.

Simon had moved on again towards the edge of the wood, and Meg reluctantly ran to catch up with him. The field wall they had been following petered out in a rubble of stones, but there was a wall on the lower side now, dividing the wood from the moor. Just before they reached the trees they heard the sound again, longer this time and ending in a drawn-out wail that faded to nothing but a trembling of the air. Meg's sense of foreboding grew stronger. The sound seemed to be coming from the clough – and that was where she was supposed to be safe.

16

THE HEART OF THE WOOD

The wood was upon them now. Meg could see beech and birch, with scrub oak and elder beneath them spilling over the broken top of the wall onto the path. And, standing like a sentinel as they approached, a huge ash with large, ungainly limbs coming off in every direction. She could hear the chuckle of water – not enough to call a stream, just a runnel draining down off the moor, cutting a little V-shaped notch in the hillside. The path led across it on planks.

Gaffer had taught her a lot about trees. "Ash needs a lot of water," he said. "He puts his roots down deep. You don't want him near where you grow things; he'll dry the soil out. He's good for making tools, and the old spears were always made of ash. You can use the young tips and leaves for an adder's bite too. And he's the best there is for burning. Many's the load of ash I've carted round for them as were willing to pay for it." Then he would put another log on the fire.

These trees were denser than the outlying sycamores, and the beeches, in particular, were much taller. High branches arched over them, enfolding them, making them part of the wood. The silence here was deeper, heavier than it had been in the open, and the gurgling of water from below sounded hollow, as though it were running through a cave.

A cold shiver made its way down Meg's back. Someone walking over your grave, Mother called it. It reminded Meg of the graves in the churchyard. How many times had she walked over them? The thought of somebody walking over her grave made her shiver again. Or was it the weather? It was definitely colder than it had been; it was now late afternoon, and the sun had gone behind a cloud. Even so, it shouldn't be as chilly as this, she thought. Simon must have noticed it too because he stopped, undid his bag and took out a jerkin.

"I got this from one of the grooms. You have it," he said, handing it to her. "At least I've got a doublet." It was too big, but she was grateful for it.

Meg began to feel strange. The shiver was now crawling across her scalp, making it tingle and causing the hairs on her neck to stand on end. She knew that feeling; there was something watching her – something in the wood.

She was frightened to look, but her gaze was drawn to the shadows among the trees, darker blobs among the dark trunks. She couldn't see the ground because it fell away too steeply, and there was mist rising. Mist? You didn't expect mist on a day like this. It was creeping above the level of the boundary wall as though a breathing dragon lay below.

She watched in horrified fascination as a tendril of mist detached itself from the rest and began to coil round the trunk of one of the beech trees, like a living thing snaking its way up into the branches. It was happening on other trees too. The mist spread out when it reached the top, like ragged clouds combed by the topmost twigs.

Meg could feel it grow colder still as they approached the steps which led to the cottage. Maybe running down them would warm her up. They could only see the top few; how many were there?

One, two, three steps down and Meg felt she was about to be swallowed up in mist and silence. The sense of somebody or something watching her became overpowering. There were fierce eyes out there, watching, waiting; pinpoints of light that seemed to penetrate the mist and bore into her skull. What for? What did they want to do? She stared into the trees, her eyes sore, not daring to blink in case she missed some vital signal, something that would mean the difference between surviving and being plunged into some unknown horror.

Then she became aware of a quite different sensation. The bag at her waist was moving. She remembered how Bolly-Bolly had jumped when she'd first seen a movement on the hillside. Now he wanted to get out and was rolling about inside the bag in a rage. She slackened the drawstring, and pulled Bolly-Bolly out. She wasn't sure whether he was frightened or angry, but he was staring into the wood as well – shaking even more now. She needed two hands to keep hold of him.

When she looked up, Simon was no longer in front of her. He must have lost his sense of direction and gone off the steps. Meg caught a glimpse of him before he disappeared from view. With increasing alarm, she heard him cry, then the noise of him crashing or falling as he gathered pace, freewheeling down the slope out of control. Surely he must hit a tree and knock himself cold.

As if in answer to her thought, the noise stopped, replaced by an ominous silence. Meg's own mind was clear now. And the mist seemed to have cleared a little too. She held on to Bolly-Bolly and ran down the steps in search of Simon, expecting to see him stretched out on the ground.

She found his bag first, snagged on a thorn bush. She hitched it over her shoulder and hurried on.

A little further, the steps turned abruptly right and became less steep. She could make out the vague shape of a cottage below her, with thick smoke rising from its roof. Was it smoke and not mist that had obscured her view? Surely not; she would have smelled it as she could now – smoke from dry, well-seasoned wood. She watched it rise up, hardly touching the trees at all.

Then, to her left, inside a clump of holly bushes, she noticed a thick, swirling patch of fog. It was dense and dark, as though all the mist in the wood had concentrated in one place. She knew that was where Simon was. She gripped Bolly-Bolly tightly and plunged down into it.

Meg felt she had been wrenched out of her own world and into the realms of nightmare. She was surrounded by swirling mist like a moving, circular wall, but, within that space the air was clear, though there was a suffocating smell of brimstone that made it difficult to breathe.

Simon was pinned to the ground by a monstrous bear-like figure that crouched over him, its front feet with long, extended claws forcing his shoulders down. Simon was gasping for air, moving his head from side to side as he tried to prevent his face from being buried in the creature's underbelly as it bore down on him.

Meg tried to take a step forward but found herself unable to move. Instead she was forced to watch, helpless, as Bolly-Bolly slipped from her nerveless grasp onto the ground.

Was this one of Simon's visions that she had somehow been dragged into? It seemed both real and unreal. The wood was real, she had seen it from afar and come down the steps; she had put out her hand and felt trunks and branches. Even now, though she couldn't move, she could feel the pricking of dead holly leaves under her feet.

But what about the hideous hairy thing that seemed to be trying to suffocate the life out of Simon? She willed herself to believe that it was just an illusion

– but she could smell it! A hot, animal stink teased her nostrils.

It raised its head and stared at her. Its face was hairless and strangely human. It had a long, sharp nose, dark, piercing eyes close together and a large mouth that twisted in an ugly sneer. It shifted position, pulling its body upright, which allowed Simon to breathe more easily; he stopped thrashing around and Meg could see the rapid rise and fall of his chest. The creature looked less like a bear now; its legs were long and thin. Its chest and belly were covered with pale hair, and there were two, four, six pairs of teats dangling flat and empty like a dried-up sow's. It stalked across the clearing towards her.

She felt under attack even before the creature reached her; something was trying to probe into her mind. She tried to pick up Bolly-Bolly, but the spell that prevented her from moving was still there. She couldn't even scream.

The creature stood in front of her now, its face only inches away; its intense gaze boring into her. Its rancid smell was overpowering, catching the back of her throat and making her eyes water. She expected every moment to see it lunge forward, to feel the hard, painful grip of its claws as it caught her and bore her to the ground, intent on smothering the life out of her.

Instead, it opened its mouth. At first it seemed like a malignant laugh, but the thin, bloodless lips went on stretching and the gap between them grew wider and wider – impossibly wide, as though its head were splitting in two – and another creature emerged from its throat. This one's face was dominated by huge fangs. Its eyes were whirling circles of red and it had long, pointed ears, tufted at the ends.

A chill of recognition ran through Meg. When she had been a little girl there had been pictures on the church walls, before the Puritans had insisted they be whitewashed over. That's where she'd seen a head like this before – it belonged to a demon who dragged souls off to hell, the entrance to which was the gaping mouth of a huge fish, and you could see more demons and fire inside it.

The demon came right out and was fully visible now. It had hoofed feet, a pointed tail, and carried a large trident. This couldn't be real, but the intention of the demon was plain enough: it was going to impale her body on its trident and pitchfork her into the creature's mouth, the mouth of hell, whatever it was. And that would be the end of her. She was certain that her life – her real life – was in danger. This wasn't just a vision conjured out of the air, or put there by some harmless magic. This was evil and threatening and it was going to kill her. This was the death heralded by the Skriker she had seen and heard on the hillside – if that's what it was, if that hadn't just been conjured too – not her father's death, but *hers*, here and now.

Her body couldn't react to the terror that swept through her mind. She felt detached from it, as though her spirit had already left, ripped from her physical self, destined to wander restless, unable to be at peace. She was overwhelmed by helpless, hopeless despair.

But not entirely. A tiny corner of her mind was still aware of the clearing, the trees, the mist, the shadowed fastness of the wood. And the wood was disturbed by the intruding presence as she was; she could sense a troubled movement among the limbs and branches. Like the ghosts in the graveyard, tree spirits couldn't move far. They could flit around their trees and you could sometimes catch a glimpse of them, but they wouldn't venture into the heart of the clearing. Only the hollies that surrounded her – the guardians of the clearing – seemed immune to the general perturbation, to the uneasy quivering of the leaves and the agitated rustling in the undergrowth.

She became aware of Simon too. The creature had

left him prostrate on the ground, but Meg knew he was stirring; through the agony of her own torment, she saw him rise like a pale ghost from the forest floor. The demon saw him. It gave a grunt of surprise, and Meg sensed its irritation at being interrupted. In a fit of petulance it turned its attention away from her, and she collapsed to the ground. It raised its trident and flung it at Simon.

But Simon wasn't going to be dispatched so easily. He rushed forward and dropped to the ground as the trident flew over his head and stuck in the soft earth behind him. With a yelp of annoyance, the demon bounded over him and tugged it out.

Simon rushed to Meg, his eyes fixed on the ground beside her, and scooped up something in his hands.

"I don't know what you can do with him, but you've got to do something!" he said, handing Bolly-Bolly to her. The demon was upon him already, holding the trident above him with two hands, intending to jab it down and stick him like a pig. As the prongs came down he rolled out of their way, over and over in the dead leaves.

The demon screamed with frustration and rage as the weapon buried itself halfway up the shaft. By the time it had wrenched it free, Simon had scrambled to his feet and was running across the clearing. Meg felt the demon's influence rolling away from her like the mist in the trees as it pursued Simon with the determination of someone driven to distraction by a buzzing fly.

Bolly-Bolly felt hot. This was the time – if at all – to call upon the deeper power that Ned had mentioned and which she had always sensed was there.

A stirring began inside Bolly-Bolly, a deep vibration that seemed to come from every fibre of his gnarled and twisted form. Meg concentrated her mind on that and willed him into action. A sense of the ancient power she was unleashing flooded over her. It was like being in the presence of something so immense that you could never see or know its extent, but at the same time you could hold it in the palm of your hand, like a seed. She began to tremble as she felt power coursing through her, linking with that which was throbbing inside Bolly-Bolly.

With a jerk, he tore free from her grasp. He hung in the air for a moment and she could see his eyes blazing with an intense fire that seemed bottomless. Then a blinding flash lit up the clearing, and a horse, half the height of the trees, reared on its hind legs, snorting and pawing the air. It was richly dressed with red and gold trappings, and on its back a woman in silver armour sat holding a lance that pointed straight at the demon.

The demon had reached the edge of the clearing, but it turned from its pursuit of Simon and faced the woman, its three-pronged fork held aloft. There was an odd moment of stillness before the two opposing forces charged at each other. Lance met trident and a colossal crack shook the trees as a ball of searing brightness shot upwards and crashed through the canopy, shredding the mist as it went. With a splintering crash, the top part of a birch tree fell, smouldering, until it caught in the lower branches and hung like a broken mast in the shrouds of a storm-tossed ship.

Meg blinked her eyes to banish the swirling after-images of the flash. The horse, now a more normal size, came into view again. It was standing quietly, while its rider held her lance down with the demon squirming and squealing feebly on the end. It shrank, then wriggled free of the point of the lance and flew up into the mouth from which it had emerged. The creature faded, losing substance, until it was nothing more than a dark shadow melting noiselessly away among the trees. For a moment, Meg thought she saw the figure of a man, but the image was soon gone.

The woman looked at Meg. She wasn't young, and though there was triumph in her bearing, her face had a grim, battle-hardened look to it, and there was concern in her deeply furrowed brow. Meg thought she might have been going to speak, but she seemed to decide against it, and wheeled her horse's head round with a tug of the rein. With a final flourish of her lance in Meg's direction, she moved off into the trees until all that Meg could see was her shining armour, then that faded too and she was gone.

Meg took in her surroundings again. It was gloomy in the wood, but not dark. The sun still hadn't set, though it must be quite late in the evening by now. The clearing was almost perfectly circular, and most of the trees were of a similar size and age. Had the hollies grown round it by chance or had they been deliberately planted – a special place in the heart of the wood?

She felt the grip of its magic. It wasn't wholly dark, though dark things had been happening here. But that darkness had been brought in from outside and she had seen it go. It had been using this space, tapping into the magic here for its own ends, but it didn't belong here.

Meg knew that she and Bolly-Bolly had used that magic too. It was like a window into the ancient time; if you could open it just a little, then the power and the magic came flooding in – as it had in the moment when Bolly-Bolly had leaped from her hands. They had proved stronger than the foul creature that attacked her and Simon – this time – but Meg didn't think it had gone for ever.

Bolly-Bolly lay on the ground beside her. She picked him up, and he felt like nothing more than a dead piece of wood, as though all the power had drained out of him. Would it come back again – or not? It was a dreadful thought, and she held him close in her hands like a frozen bird, desperately hoping she could bring him back.

She put him carefully in the bag and tried to stand. But now her own weakness engulfed her. She could hardly struggle to her knees. Whether it was the attention of the demon or her own efforts that had drained her of strength she didn't know, but she felt dizzy and sick. She made another attempt to get to her feet, but it made her head swim and her sight blur. She felt herself tottering, and couldn't stop herself falling face down onto the ground. The last thing she remembered was the taste of earth in her mouth.

* * *

Simon, trembling with relief and aching all over, left the shelter of the beech tree where he had crouched to witness the conflict. Images of the creature, the demon, the shining figure were still swirling in his mind. It had been more than an ordinary vision.

He had just come to the conclusion that it was all over, when he saw Meg fall. Was this the demon's parting shot? He ran to her, ignoring the pains shooting up his legs from being cramped, and turned her onto her back.

She was still and pale, and her free arm flopped to the ground. His heart skipped a beat and he kneeled down beside her. He put his cheek to her lips and, for a panic-filled moment he thought she wasn't breathing. Then he felt it; light, rapid and shallow. He let out a pent-up breath of his own.

Should she be left where she was, to recover in her own time? It might be better to move her, get her away from the remnants of the dark influence that still lingered in the clearing. He needed help. There was only the cottage nearby; he hoped Hal's mother would know what to do. He didn't like to leave Meg alone, but it would only be for a few minutes.

He made his way down the remaining steps as

quickly as he could, to the cottage at the bottom. Its timbers and roof thatch were moss-covered and it almost seemed to be part of the hillside, like some strange natural growth. The door was open. He knocked and peered in.

The reek of smoke was strong, and it was hard to see anything, but there was movement inside.

"Who is it?" The voice sounded surprised, suspicious. She wouldn't be used to visitors.

"I'm Simon Jolly," he said. "Are you Hal's mother?"

"Aye. Lizzie Walker. What's up? You're all out of breath. Has something happened to him?"

"No...no. He sent us here." Simon made an effort to steady himself.

"Us? Is there more than one o' yer?"

"No – I mean yes... Meg needs help. She had...an accident in the woods. Please come!" He hoped she wouldn't want a full explanation just yet.

Lizzie moved into the light. She was thin and bent, but must have been a big woman, once. Her hands were huge, like Hal's, though they were more knotted and twisted. She took a good look at him and seemed satisfied.

"Come on then," she said. "I can see you're worried. You can tell me about it later."

Simon turned and hurried off up the steps, with Lizzie right on his heels, showing surprising energy for someone so old.

The mist had dispersed entirely now, and the last of the sun had found a gap in the treetops left by the fallen birch. A ray of light, pointing like a finger, lanced into the clearing, though it couldn't dispel the uneasiness that still haunted the place. The sunbeam lit up Meg's body, still lying where he had left her – but she wasn't alone. Simon caught his breath and nearly stumbled. A dark figure was bending over her.

Why had he left her? He had been so concerned to get help that he hadn't considered whether the evil might return. He thought it had been defeated, but it had simply waited until she was alone and come back again – this time in human form.

"There's somebody there already," Lizzie said, moving ahead of Simon and peering through the trees. "He'll be able to help us take your friend down to the cottage."

"No, no!" Simon put out his arm to try and stop Lizzie, but he was too late. His hand clutched on empty air as the old woman darted forward into the clearing. Simon braced himself as the figure unbent and slowly turned towards them.

It was a man, not very tall, dressed in black, with close-cropped grey hair, and he was holding the Complete Herbal – he must have come across Simon's bag. His expression was grave, but not unfriendly. Certainly not suffused with hate and malice, which is what Simon expected.

"Good afternoon," he said, and gave them a slight bow. "I'm sorry if I startled you."

Lizzie must have been pleased to be treated with such civility and kept walking towards the man, but Simon was still wary – polite gentlemen were not always what they seemed, if you believed the old stories. It was easy to be deceived by a smooth tongue.

"Who...who are you?" he asked, fear and uncertainty gnawing inside him.

"Mmm?" The man raised one eyebrow. "Haven't you recognized me yet? I know my appearance has changed, but..."

Simon peered at the man, and the shock of recognition made him weak at the knees.

"Dr. Challenor!"

17

THE CRYSTAL EYE

Meg came round to the sharp smell of vinegar – and something else – at the back of her nose. It trickled down into her throat and almost became a taste. She opened her mouth and took a deep breath, taking in more of the fumes, which set her coughing.

Her eyes were streaming, and she struggled to open them. She wasn't in the clearing any longer, but lying on the floor at one end of a dim room, looking at two people she didn't know. One was an old woman holding a cloth to her nose.

When she saw Meg open her eyes, she gave an exclamation of satisfaction. "Ah! I knew that would do the trick." She passed a bottle to a man standing beside her. "Dwarf Elder infused in vinegar, with a few spices. Can't beat it for reviving folk. Better than all your volatile salts."

The man took a sniff, recoiled at the pungency of it, then nodded his approval and handed it back. The woman poured a little more onto the cloth, moved behind Meg, and set to rubbing her temples with it.

Meg could now see that Simon was behind the man, standing beside a stone fireplace and looking anxious.

"Who...who are..."

Meg's question was intended for Simon, but the woman answered. "I'm Lizzie Walker, Hal's mother. And this gentleman's an apothecary called Dr. Challenor – your friend's old master."

"Dr. Challenor? But how...?"

"Don't you fret yourself about that just now. Let's revive you properly first."

Dr. Challenor – and it must be him if Simon said so – didn't look at all as Meg had expected. She had imagined someone tall, commanding, with flowing hair and beard, dressed in outlandish robes, but here he was; short-haired, dressed in a black doublet and breeches, black hose and shoes with flat ribbon fastenings. Only the lack of a collar, and slashed sleeves showing flashes of dusky pink from his shirt underneath, broke the dull, formal impression.

He kneeled beside her on one knee and looked at her more closely. There was something about his face that was deep and serious; even when he looked straight at her, his eyes seemed to be looking into the far distance.

Meg tried to sit up.

"You lie still, lass," Lizzie said, patting her head. "I'll make you a little something to soothe you." She stirred the fire with a poker, giving life to a tongue of red flame, and a plume of blue-grey smoke that spiralled up to the roof where it hung, briefly, before making its way out through a hole. Then she took a jug from the table and handed it to Simon. "We'll get some water from the beck, then you can help me find some fresh camomile," she said, as she led him out of the cottage.

Now that Lizzie's concoction was no longer near her nose, Meg could detect other smells. There was woodsmoke, of course, the sharp tang of cured fleeces, the slightly rancid smell of hanging bacon, and a sweeter scent that reminded Meg of new-mown hay. Her eyes were more accustomed to the dim interior now, and she could see bunches of dried and drying herbs hanging from the low roof beams. A loom stood in front of the only window, much like Father's, only smaller. There was a spinning wheel too, in front of the fire, with a basket of wool and the room's only chair. It looked to have been roughly hewn from a single trunk, and Meg wondered whether it was Hal's work. It had a high back, curved round to form sides that would keep out winter draughts.

Meg's eyes kept straying to Dr. Challenor. She couldn't imagine what had brought him here – other than some magic she didn't understand.

"Let's prop you up a bit," he said, and rolled up one of the fleeces that lay on the floor and pushed it under her shoulders. She could see the other end of the room now. A short ladder led up to a raised platform with a mattress on it. Under the platform were shelves containing all manner of jars, bottles, boxes and bundles.

Dr. Challenor sat in the chair, which he had moved round until it faced her. He was studying her again with those intense and distant eyes, though there was a bit of a twinkle in them.

"Simon's told me a lot about you," she said.

A half smile played about his lips. "That may – or may not – be a good thing. But at least I won't be like a complete stranger."

"He said you might be in prison – or even dead."

His smile broadened. "I escaped both those fates, fortunately. As you can see, I'm very much alive – though rather changed in appearance. When you move in the circles that I did, it's easy to make enemies. Some of my former clients were prominent churchmen – which didn't endear me to the Puritans. Others were courtiers, which had the same effect. All they needed to pursue me, was an excuse. When someone I'd been treating had the misfortune to die of something quite unrelated, they had it. I was accused of witchcraft."

"You? But—"

"Yes, I know you were too. Simon told me. He knows it's safe to confide in me. I know how it feels. But your father is in gaol and may be unjustly condemned to death, and neither of us knows how *that* feels. I don't know much about the circumstances yet, but I want to assure you that I will do everything in my power to help your father."

"But that's not why you came here, is it?"

Dr. Challenor's face became serious. "No, it isn't. I don't want to disturb you even more, but I can't avoid what I have to say, and I can't make light of it. I came in response to the imminent danger that faces *you*. I first had wind of it when you were in the hayloft earlier today, looking at my Complete Herbal. I live in York now, but today I happened to be at Mirfield in search of a lost manuscript, and close enough to see you – I'll tell you how in a minute. I rode in all haste to Halifax, only to find that you'd fled and the whole town seemed to be searching for you. Fortunately, you were near enough for me to see where you were, and have some sense of its whereabouts.

"I thought I might be too late, but your device intervened before the worst could happen. I'm not convinced that whatever it was – let's call it the adversary – intended to kill you, despite what you might have felt at the time. A holly clearing is not a place of death; you might be taken to the point between life and death, but not beyond. There are places—"

"But why was it attacking me? What did it want?" The question was out before Meg had time to think. She thought Dr. Challenor might chide her for her impatience, but he didn't seem to mind the interruption.

"I think it sensed your power – as I did – and wanted to find some way of using it for its own ends."

"And what would have happened if Bolly-Bolly hadn't stopped it?"

"Who knows how long your torment would have continued? And Simon may have been dead once he stepped out of the holly grove. I might have arrived in time to prevent these things, or I might not."

Meg felt a stab of guilt that Simon had once again been put in danger because of her, though thankful that she – or rather Bolly-Bolly – had been the means of saving him.

"Your device certainly has surprising power," Dr. Challenor said, leaning towards her. "Would you..." He seemed hesitant, as if he was asking a great favour. "Would you allow me a closer look – as one Maker to another?"

So she had been right about Dr. Challenor – he was a Maker, and he knew that she was too. She had never expected to meet him, but now there was a growing excitement inside her. She hadn't really had time to take in what being a Maker meant. She understood what Ned had said, but it hadn't yet become part of the way she thought about herself. But now, just to be in the presence of someone with the knowledge and wisdom of Dr. Challenor, and for him to talk to her, set her pulse racing. Of course she didn't mind. She took Bolly-Bolly out of the bag and passed him over.

"He's not a device," she said, hoping Dr. Challenor

wouldn't be too disappointed. "He's just one of my figures."

That hint of a smile returned to one corner of his mouth. "And all the more remarkable for that."

He didn't run his hands over Bolly-Bolly's surface, as Ned had done, instead he stared intently at him, looking into his eyes as Meg did.

"What do *you* have – as one Maker to another?" Meg asked. She wondered if she were being too bold, but Dr. Challenor undid the top buttons of his doublet, put his hand in the front of his shirt and brought out something hanging on a chain around his neck.

"I'm afraid I cannot think of this as anything other than a device. Probably because I had no hand in its making."

When he opened his fist, Meg gasped. Hanging from the chain by a silver mount in the shape of a claw, was a ball, about the size of a small egg, but perfectly round. It appeared to be made of glass, which sparkled and twinkled in the soft light of the lamp. It was clear and flawless, and, in the centre, another sphere of equal clarity floated, its outline winking in and out of vision as the wavering light caught and lost it. And in the centre of that, was something irregular in shape; dark red, nearly black and about the size of Meg's little fingernail, though it was hard to tell because the curved glass distorted it. She couldn't tell what it was – a piece of rock or semi-precious stone? It seemed to be suspended, held there by some invisible force or power. She knew there was magic deep within it, radiating from its heart.

Meg thought Dr. Challenor's "device" was the most wondrous object she had ever seen.

"This is my far-seeing eye," Dr. Challenor said. "It may look different from yours, and no doubt they work in different ways, but they share the same magic."

"But Bolly-Bolly's only a piece of wood. This...this is..."

"Only a piece of wood too. It may be encased in a double crystal sphere, but it, too, began life as part of a tree."

Meg looked intently at the fragment at the heart of the spheres. It didn't look like a piece of wood, it looked too hard and shiny. "But it's not an ordinary piece of wood, not like Bolly-Bolly. Someone just chopped him off a tree."

"It is only a matter of age. This piece came from part of a tree that had lain buried in a peat bog for thousands of years. I cannot tell you what kind of tree it was, maybe a species that no longer exists, but those who found it knew its ancient magic, unlike your woodcutter. When it dried out they broke it into pieces, each one treasured at the time. Some were formed into rings and other small objects, but I don't know of another like this. Many have been lost, or destroyed by those who fear the power they contain.

"How many remain, I don't know. It took me many years and much travelling to track this one down, and a small fortune to make it mine. And yet..." He shook his head slowly and looked at Bolly-Bolly again. "And yet here is an object of recently living wood hacked from a tree, which has the power of the Ancients in it as truly and certainly as this; a Woodenface that has carried its spark of life through generations of hawthorn trees waiting for someone like you to release it." Beams of light flashed from the spheres as he twirled the chain between his fingers.

"But your eye must have more power than Bolly-Bolly."

"Why? Because it's exquisitely fashioned and flashes in the light? How easily we are seduced by appearance."

"But you are..."

"I am Will Challenor. I may be called doctor, mage, apothecary, physician, astrologer, alchemist, even wizard, but all those titles are to do with how other people see me, and they refer to my learning and experience, not who I am. I do have some natural talent – I am a Maker, though not one of the most gifted – but as for the rest, it all has to do with circumstance, opportunity and my capacity to learn.

"You have more natural ability than I have, but it's untamed and unpredictable. It shines out of you like a beacon for those who can see. Even those who cannot, many of them, know there is something unusual, strange, even frightening about you.

"When I saw you through the Crystal Eye, looking at my book with Simon this morning, I knew that my journey to Mirfield had been no mere chance. There are some aspects of far-seeing that even I do not understand, but the Crystal Eye had sensed you – and your...Bolly-Bolly – before I had the opportunity to see you, and drew me to you like a knife to a lodestone."

The door sneck clicked and Lizzie and Simon came in. Dr. Challenor put the Crystal Eye away, and Meg put Bolly-Bolly back in the bag. She didn't think it mattered if Lizzie saw him, but she was beginning to understand why she must be careful. Lizzie poured some water from the jug into a pot on the hearth and tossed in the herbs she had brought, then hung the pot over the fire on the sway-cleek.

Meg was dumbfounded by what Dr. Challenor had said about her. She could hardly recognize herself; it was like looking in the smooth surface of a pond and finding someone else staring up at you.

And he knew how special Bolly-Bolly was, too. She wished he'd been able to say more about the power that was present in both Bolly-Bolly and the Crystal Eye. She would have liked to hold the Eye in her hands and stare into its depths, as Dr. Challenor had done with Bolly-Bolly. What would she discover? It was hard to believe that such a beautiful object was no more powerful than Bolly-Bolly – he could be so awkward at times.

Lizzie produced a three-legged stool from under the table, and insisted Simon sat on it, though he tried to persuade her to take the weight from her own legs.

"I can't be sitting down while there are guests standing," she said, and found space for the stool between the woodpile and the hearth.

Meg suspected that Lizzie didn't do much sitting down at all, except to weave and spin. She had the air of someone who was constantly busy. She fetched a ladle, and, after a few vigorous stirs, took some of the infusion from the pot and poured it into a mug, which she brought to Meg and held to her lips. The smell and taste of camomile were familiar and comforting. Meg hadn't realized how thirsty she was.

A knock at the door made her jump. It was followed by another, accompanied by a voice.

"I'm Ned Fletcher. Is this where Lizzie Walker lives?"

"He's one of us," Simon said. Lizzie gave him a wary look, but went to open the door.

Meg's heart hammered in her chest. So Ned had found them. Surely he would bring news of Father.

18

ANOTHER THREAT

"Will Challenor? Zounds!" Ned enclosed Dr. Challenor in a huge embrace, then slapped his back as though he had a piece of gristle lodged in his gullet.

"How long is it since we met? Not since I was an actor, I'll be bound. Always one for the plays, eh?" Ned stepped back and looked Dr. Challenor over. "But how you've changed! Long flowin' locks you used to have, and ever dressed in fashion. I remember once at a performance of *The Changeling* – I was playing Franciscus, the counterfeit madman, as you may recall – a gentleman of the audience complained as he couldn't see beyond the ostrich plume in your cocked hat. Quite irate he got, until a wag shouts out, 'Well, you ain't missin' much!' Drew more laughs

227

than the play, I must confess. An' look at you now. You'd pass for a Roundhead, so you would."

Dr. Challenor opened his mouth to speak, but Ned was in full flow. "Time ain't doin' none of us no favours, though, is it? Hair turns grey – or falls out entire – skin wrinkles and knees creak. But, there's one thing I'll be eternally grateful to you for, Will." He put a hand on Dr. Challenor's shoulder. "D'you remember when I was passin' blood? You gave me a decoction of clown's woundwort and comfrey root in wine, and since that day my water's been as clear as a mountain stream."

"What's happened to Father?" Meg's voice brought a sudden halt to Ned's prolonged greeting, and an awkward silence fell. She had the feeling that he'd been deliberately talking about other things, putting off the moment when he would have to tell her what he knew.

Ned dropped his arm, and his shoulders sagged. He took off his cap and wiped sweat from his forehead with it.

"I wish as I could say it was good news, but it ain't." His voice had lost all its joviality and he seemed to have shrunk. Whereas before he had appeared to fill all available space in the small cottage, now his presence was less. He perched himself on the bench of Lizzie's loom and looked downcast. "The court condemned him. He's due to be 'headed tomorrow. Me an' Nan did what we could, but the steward wouldn't let us in – said Nan wasn't a fit an' proper person to give evidence. They'd hired ruffians with dogs an' staves to keep the crowd back. I expect you want to hear the detail of what led up to it," he said to Dr. Challenor and Lizzie. "But that's best comin' from Meg."

Meg didn't want to say anything, and found it difficult to tell her story without breaking down. But collecting her thoughts and trying to explain what had happened in a way that made sense to her listeners, helped her to put her mind to Father's trouble rather than be swept away by the emotion of it. She couldn't see Lizzie's face, at the back of the room, but Dr. Challenor listened intently, his brows drawn and his mouth set.

When she'd finished, Ned took over again, pulling his gown round him and planting his feet firmly on the floor.

"There was nothin' left for us to do but go back all gloomy like an' ponder on what might ha' been. But when we gets to town, there's a buzz about this witch girl what's wanted. Daughter o' John Lumb what's just been condemned. When I asks as to what she's supposed to ha' done, it seems she brought grievous injury to two prominent yeomen by causin' them to fly off o' the gibbet platform an' land in a heap at the bottom!"

"That was me!" Simon jumped up from his stool, almost indignant. "I pushed them off."

"That's not the tale that's goin' round, is it? Everyone says it's the witch girl. And then, they say, she robbed 'em – took everything they had."

"Robbed them? I did see someone bending over them as I went to the Cross – a young man. I thought he was helping them. What made them think it was Meg?"

"She makes them fly off – she robs them. Follows, don't it?"

"But they can't have seen her."

"Seems they didn't see nothin' after they fell, not until there was a whole bunch o' people round 'em. Witch stole their memories, see? And her father a condemned cloth stealer. Some said the whole family should be exterminated – sorry, I shouldn't ha' told you that. It just shows how a crowd can turn."

Meg felt bewildered. "How can people be like that?"

Ned shrugged. "They're frightened. They see things

goin' on what they don't understand, an' they've got to have somebody to blame. If they don't see how it happened, it must be a witch. An' they're frightened o' witches, 'cos a witch might just put a spell on 'em if she don't like what they says or what they does. Sense an' reason goes out the window when you're talkin' about witches."

Meg found some comfort in the fact that Simon was now free of suspicion, despite being the culprit. At least he could go back to Halifax without fear of arrest. She didn't mind taking the blame – there were so many other things she'd been accused of.

"I did have another idea," Ned said. "I thought me an' Hal could go tonight an' pinch the blade. They can't chop his head off if they ain't got no blade, an' Hal made it in the first place! But, o' course, the blade ain't there. Some says it's off for sharpenin', others says they never set it up until the mornin' o' the gibbetin' anyways."

Nobody said anything. Ned stood up, slackened the drawstrings of his money bag and took out a penny.

"Seems like we ain't got no more options." He spun the penny in the air and caught it as it fell. He turned it over on the back of his hand and held it out to Meg. "Tails they win, heads you lose."

Meg looked at the face of the king staring up at her from the back of Ned's hand. Cromwell and his men had chopped his head off too. Thousands of people hadn't wanted that to happen. But they weren't able to stop it.

"We have to save him," she said in a whisper, hoping it sounded as though she meant it, because inside her there was a deep well of hopelessness. She wasn't at the bottom of it yet, but every minute that went by brought her nearer.

Ned walked over to the fire, and put another log on, pushing it in with his foot. A shower of sparks cascaded up to the roof in the near dark. He lit a taper and put it to a rushlight that sat on a shelf above the chair. Threatening shadows leaped round the walls and across the underside of the roof. It was easy to imagine a looming gibbet or the exaggerated features of a sharp-nosed face. A mood of depression was settling on them.

"Can you do anythin'?" Ned asked Dr. Challenor. "Can you spell him free?"

"You have an exaggerated notion of my abilities, Ned," Dr. Challenor replied. "I work with nature, not against it. I cannot merely utter magic words and have the prisoner walk through the walls of the gaol, or command the gibbet blade to halt in its descent. I wish..."

"Whose testimony condemned him, then?"

Meg jumped. She had almost forgotten about Lizzie back there in the shadows. Now they had a light, Meg could just see her sitting at the bottom of the steps that led up to her bed. Lizzie stood up and moved forward into the circle of brighter light cast by the lamp.

"It was Edgar Womersley's apprentice, Toby Gledhill," Ned said. "Sutcliffe's behind it all. He's the one as wants John Lumb executed. But it was Womersley's cloth what was supposed to be stolen." He stood to one side, back to the wall, as Lizzie sat on the bench.

"It's false testimony, then?"

"O' course it is. It's all to feed a private grudge."

"Testimony can be changed, you know. I remember when I were a lass, there was one due to be 'headed. They had him on the block, and, at the last minute, the witness changed his mind. Couldn't bear the thought of hellfire and damnation for sending an innocent man to his death."

Ned gave a mirthless laugh. "The punishments o' Sutcliffe an' Womersley is more real to young Toby than hell an' damnation, I reckon. He's still a boy."

Meg knew what it was like to be frightened of grown-ups, but she also knew that the way you felt about it didn't always remain the same. There might be something you wanted to say but didn't dare, unless you felt safe, unless you knew there was somebody who wouldn't let the worst happen to you.

"Toby would tell the truth if he wasn't scared of Womersley," she said. "Couldn't we look after him? If he said that Sutcliffe and Womersley made him tell those lies, then they would be tried and put in gaol, wouldn't they? And Toby wouldn't have to worry any more."

Ned was doubtful. "But how does we get hold of Toby? He won't be paradin' round town, will he? An' we can't go up to Womersley's place an' say 'Please can we talk to Toby?' He'll be kept somewheres well out o' the way."

"But we can demand to see him," Simon said, and it really sounded as though he thought it was possible. There was a light in his eye.

But Ned didn't notice. "Demand? Who's goin' to take any notice of us?"

"It depends who you mean by 'us'. We'll need some help. I was thinking of someone big and strong.

234

Someone you wouldn't say no to in a hurry. Someone like—"

"Hal!" Suddenly Ned was a changed person. "M' boy, I do believe you've got it!" He rubbed his hands together and did a little jig. "We send up Hal and a few of his friends; they offer Toby protection an' bring him back. An' he makes a public declaration retractin' his evidence, in front of all them what's gathered to witness the 'headin'. I can't wait to see Sutcliffe's face. We'll have to be there early in the mornin'. Things to do; people to see."

"The youngsters can stay here till it's all over," Lizzie said.

Meg felt herself growing hot and indignant. Did everyone think she was helpless? Simon didn't look best pleased either.

"I'm coming too," she said. "You can't expect me to stay here and wait."

Ned looked doubtful. "But what if someone recognizes you?" He looked at Dr. Challenor for support, and he didn't look as though he wanted her to come either. She knew why; they only wanted to protect her, but she certainly wasn't prepared to be left behind, particularly as they had a plan that might really work. If they were going to save Father, she had to be there.

Her determination must have been written across her face, because Ned showed signs of relenting. "Well, maybe you can come as far as the smithy. You should be safe there."

That would do – for now. Once they were in Halifax who knew what might happen? Meg couldn't shift the conviction in her mind that she still had a part to play in saving her father.

"If you're going to start early you need some proper rest," Lizzie said to her. "You'd best share the bed with me. These three can manage down here. There's more fleeces under the bed if they want 'em."

Meg still felt a bit dizzy when she stood up to follow Lizzie across the room. Her mind might not want to go to sleep, but her body did.

She had just reached the steps to the bed, when there was a loud bang at the door. She stopped, her heart in her mouth. Who could it be? There were no more friends likely to come. Everyone was still, looking at each other, waiting to see if there would be another knock.

There wasn't. And no reassuring voice to put people's minds at ease.

"I'll go," Ned said in a low voice.

He took the light off the shelf and walked slowly to the door. They all listened, straining to hear any noise outside, but there was silence, apart from the rushing of the stream.

Ned opened the door and peered out into the night, holding the light up in front of him.

"No one there," he said.

He took a step out and looked around. Meg, crouching behind him, could see something white lying on the ground. Simon saw it too, took the lamp from Ned and bent down to have a closer look. He sucked in his breath and his eyes widened. "It...it's a carved head. Someone must have thrown it at the door."

Meg moved forward to see it better, but Simon pulled the lamp away quickly, almost making it go out. She took it from him and kneeled down.

The wood was very white. Meg thought it was holly; that's what it looked like when you peeled the bark off. The face had sly, calculating eyes, a large nose and a square, jutting chin. The mouth was a tight, stubborn line, and a mess of black horsehair crowned the head, making the whole face dark and sinister. You couldn't call it a likeness – at least Meg couldn't – but there was no doubt who it was meant to be. It was an image of her; an unpleasant and exaggerated image, and it made her blood run cold.

Dread grew in her belly, and gathered into a hard lump. The sense of powerlessness that had gripped her in the clearing was playing round the edges of her mind again.

Ned had seen it now, and he looked shocked. "I knows who done this. There's only one person what twists a face with that degree o' venom, an' that's Jake. But he's locked up in gaol."

"Then there must be another explanation." Dr. Challenor joined them.

"What shall we do?" Meg asked him.

"Leave it. I don't think any harm will come to you while we're all together in the house."

They went back inside and Lizzie closed the door firmly behind them.

"The entrance is good an' fast," she said. "I know the herbs that protect. And my mother had the priest in too, before I was born." She pointed to the door. Meg could see a bunch of herbs hanging over it, and two diagonal crosses carved in the jambs. "Betony and St John's Wort – and St Andrew's cross. No evil may come nigh this dwelling." She said it like a ritual chant, but it seemed to Meg that evil had already come nigh.

She was shaking now. Her feeling that the malign presence in the clearing had not gone right away had proved true. It was out there now and it was seeking her again, like a prowling wolf. It hadn't given up. Despite Dr. Challenor's and Lizzie's reassurances, Meg didn't feel safe. Just when she had something to be thankful for, some hope that they might be able to rescue Father, another threat had presented itself.

At that moment there was another bang at the door, louder and harder than the first. Whatever had been thrown had been hurled with great force. It would have broken through a flimsier door. Meg could sense the real alarm that passed through them all. A movement in the bag at her waist made her heart leap – Bolly-Bolly was stirring! He must be able to feel the dark power drawing in again, and know it was directed against her. She had been so afraid that the battle with the adversary had robbed him of his power for ever. But she still didn't know how much he'd recovered, and whether he'd be able to protect her now if she needed him to.

She felt compelled to approach the door; this was her adversary, and she couldn't expect anyone else to face it – and she still had the lamp.

"Wait!"

Meg paused.

Dr. Challenor moved forward into the circle of light. His expression was grim. "This adversary is not only powerful, but cunning. Open the door by all means – it must not think you are fearful – but be very careful."

He stood beside Meg as her thumb pushed down on the sneck. The click of it opening made her jump. The squeak of the hinges sounded like an animal in pain. She opened it a few inches and peeked out.

Again, there was nobody there, but another object had joined the carved head. When she saw it, Meg's heart leaped and her legs went like jelly. How on earth had it found its way here? And who had hurled it against Lizzie's door? It was her eyeball.

She had last seen it when Bolly-Bolly had shown her the men in the barroom. She couldn't imagine that the minister had lost it. She had seen him take great care to wrap it up and put it away in a pocket. Nor could she imagine him being mixed up in the magic that was hounding her. It was hard to imagine anyone with less magic in him. But Ned said the minister had been robbed, so maybe someone else had it. That still didn't explain how it came to be here.

Ned knew what it was; she'd described it to him

during one of their conversations in the hayloft. "Ain't you goin' to pick it up?" he said. "It's yours. You made it."

Meg bent down, stretched out her hand, then stopped. The eyes on the surface were staring at her, and there was evil in them. She knew immediately that though the eyeball had been hers, it was hers no longer. The life, the power she had given to it had been stolen; taken over. It wasn't hers to command any more. It was now answerable to the adversary.

Meg felt the shock of betrayal like a physical blow. That her eyeball, patiently carved, eye by eye over days and weeks should now be used against her, was appalling. It had been such a joy to her. She had only ever used it to watch her own family. It had seemed so innocent. But now someone, or something else had looked through it, and wanted to use the power she had given it for their own terrible ends.

Was it watching her now? Had her eyeball been thrown at the door as a temptation, in the hope that Meg would take it in so they could see and hear what went on in the cottage? Or was it a threat? – *I can see you, so don't think you can get away.*

The others were behind her, looking at it. She shut the door and leaned back.

"It isn't mine any more. Can I get it back again?" she asked Dr. Challenor.

"Not easily and not now," he said. "The adversary will not let go its hold over it while you are in such confrontation. It may be lost to you for ever."

Meg put the light down on the table as people moved away from the door. Dr. Challenor still looked grim. Was he expecting another attack? She was caught between wanting and not wanting to know. He didn't say anything – no doubt he would have done if he thought they ought to be prepared.

Lizzie had gone to bed. Meg followed up the ladder, trying to convince herself that they were safe, but part of her was dreading what the night may yet have in store.

19

POSSIBILITIES

Throughout the night Meg kept waking, starting from a half doze and hearing noises – rustlings, little cracks, shrieks that were probably owls, but sounded like the demon in her imagination. Once a huge huff of air through the roof hole sent smoke and dust whirling round the cottage and set them all coughing. But there were no more bangs at the door.

In the morning they were unscathed. Meg's feeling of dread had lifted, though she felt uneasy when Lizzie opened the door. But the carved head and the eyeball were gone, the only reminder of their presence a dent in one of the door planks.

They set off for Halifax shortly after dawn. Another fine day. The wood was no longer a place of gloom and threat. Early morning light filtered through the trees and fell in patches on the steps as they climbed up, and the birds were singing again.

At the top they found Ned's pony and Dr. Challenor's horse quietly cropping the grass where they'd been tethered.

"Why doesn't your assistant go with you?" Dr. Challenor said. "Take my horse, Simon. I'd like to walk with Meg."

Meg had assumed that she and Simon would be walking together. Dr. Challenor must have things he wanted to talk to her about.

"Well, if you're sure," Ned said. "Shouldn't take you much above an hour on the high track – plenty o' time to sort ourselves out. The 'headin's due at eleven, so I heard."

To hear Ned mention it like that, as though it was just one of the day's events, brought back Meg's feeling of hopelessness. They had plans to stop it from happening, but they weren't sure of success. It was hard to believe that something involving so many important people, and fixed for a certain time, wouldn't take place.

They would probably be preparing Father now – giving him his last breakfast. Maybe the priest was already there, praying with him, trying to persuade him to confess – which he wouldn't, because he didn't do it. Maybe Mother and Gaffer were on their way to Halifax at this moment, worried and grieving. She watched Ned and Simon ride off, through a blur of tears.

Dr. Challenor didn't say anything as they went up the hillside. Maybe he didn't want to intrude on her thoughts, and was waiting for her to speak when she was ready. It gave Meg a chance to collect herself. Halfway up they moved from shadow into sunlight, and Meg hoped that was a good omen. She tried to feel hopeful, but it was difficult.

"Do you think the plan's going to work?" she asked.

Dr. Challenor looked thoughtful. "There is reason for hope, but the plan relies entirely on this Toby Gledhill, whom none of us know. I wonder if there may be some part in this for me. Nobody knows me in Halifax, so I can move freely in the town."

Meg remembered what Dr. Challenor had said last night about doing everything he could to help Father, but she hadn't expected him to become directly involved.

"Won't they miss you back in York?" she asked.

"I hardly think my absence will be noticed. Thanks to my London friends, I have a position as tutor to two young gentlemen, but their father has taken them to London for a month, so I am free to come and go from the manor house as I wish. I'm known locally as Will Sutton – a sober and rather earnest scholar. Part of me *is* Will Sutton. I could happily spend all my time on bookish pursuits and burrowing in the past – there are such excellent libraries in York. But I do miss the more active side of my old life sometimes.

"Enough about me. I rarely find myself with a like-minded person, and never before with one so young. I know you sense and respond to the power of the Ancients through Bolly-Bolly – would you mind if we talked more about that?"

Mind? It was exactly what Meg had wished for. "I hope I understand it," she said.

"You will. In one way or another. Full understanding is hardly attained in a lifetime. It's a constant journey, and you are just beginning."

They had reached the track now, and Dr. Challenor paused, looking back across the valley before they set off along the ridge.

"Can you imagine this land before it was inhabited by man?" he asked. "Before it was grazed by animals, before these walls and hedges neatly divided one field from another, before the ground was tilled or a single tree chopped down?"

Meg tried. It was easy to suppose that what she could see had always been like that – the gentle swell of the moorland, dull green and brown even at this time of the year, the brighter green of the pastures below and the dark, mottled green of the wooded cloughs that plunged into the valley. But take away the walls and fences, take away the sheep and cattle, and you could imagine the little woods bursting out of their boundaries and scrambling up the hillsides as far as they could go, possibly right to the top, covering everything you could see.

"There'd be more trees," she said.

"Yes. And before that? Before the bare bones of the Earth were covered with living things? There was such a time."

The trees vanished from the image in Meg's mind. The rounded hump of the moor broke into sharp, jagged rocks, the valley filled with water, the sky darkened and howling winds sent torrential rain lashing across the landscape.

"Just rocks and water."

"Rocks, water – and possibilities. The Ancients,

the guardians of the possibilities, came down from the heavens into this barren chaos, to charge it with life. They were constantly striving to make that which was possible into that which actually was. Some possibilities came to be, and some did not. Others survived for a short time then faded away. Others grew, developed, came together and flourished.

"Think of the possibilities that came together in the animal world – movement, sight, hearing and other senses. Without any one of these, that fox we can see would never have existed. Without language and making we humans would still be running like the fox."

Meg watched the red pelt slink along the hillside below them and disappear into an overgrown hedge. She thought she understood what Dr. Challenor was saying, but there were still so many unanswered questions.

"So how is a Maker – like you and me," she asked, "different from somebody – anybody – who just makes things? Ned talked about the power of the Ancients and 'putting the life' in things, but there's power and life everywhere."

Dr. Challenor smiled; he seemed pleased with what she'd said. "You're right. The power of the Ancients is everywhere to be seen. But when ordinary people talk about the 'power of the Ancients', what they mean is something they consider magical, beyond the power of human beings; the possibilities that have been lost to us – if we ever had them at all. Really, though, they're the *hidden* possibilities."

"But why are they hidden?"

"I don't think there's a reason. I don't think one of the Ancients came along and said, 'Right, I'll hide this possibility – say, far-seeing – from mankind.' I think it's just the way things happened, the way they 'evolved'. But there are a few people to whom it isn't hidden. You know about far-seeing, and so do I; it's there in Bolly-Bolly, and in the Crystal Eye. It's there, because this particular possibility was locked away in the trees."

"And we know it's there?"

"That's right. I think all trees still retain a faint echo of their unfulfilled possibilities. Otherwise, even you wouldn't be able to create a life for your carvings. Any object made of wood has a character of its own, depending on what kind of tree it's come from. If the woodworker is sensitive to this, the object will have a warmth, a rightness, that springs from the material itself – a tiny scrap of magic."

"But that's not something like far-seeing. Only Bolly-Bolly has that, not my other figures." She took him out of the bag and looked at him with new eyes. Bolly-Bolly was different. He was even more special than she'd imagined. She was just beginning to reawaken all those possibilities that Dr. Challenor spoke about.

"So why does Bolly-Bolly have so much magic in him?" she asked.

"I confess I'm amazed." Dr. Challenor held out his hand and took him, then pulled out the Crystal Eye and compared them. "They could hardly be more different. Its previous owner would've had me believe that the fragment in my Crystal Eye was part of the First Tree – *Wudu*, our ancestors called it – but he was anxious to sell for a high price. True or not, there's no doubting the fragment's extreme age. I had always thought that such magic – those possibilities waiting to be ignited – could only be found in ancient wood, close to the beginning, when the possibilities were still new.

"I've seen several Woodenfaces on my travels, but they were all old – a mask worn by a shaman in a ritual dance to communicate with the gods; a carved head on a pole carried round at seed time to bring fertility to the crops. I've even seen one or two said to be figures of Christ. But never anything like your Bolly-Bolly. Where did he come from?" he asked, handing him back.

Meg thought of the solitary hawthorn left standing by the woodcutters; the blood on the wound where Bolly-Bolly had been sliced off. He had looked both ways; down to the roots and up to the branches – the most magical part of the tree – but she was sure that the rest of the tree held ancient magic too. And she wasn't the only one. She thought about the little gifts left beside it.

"He came from a special tree," she said.

"I don't doubt it. We shouldn't be too surprised. No matter how long removed from the First Tree, there is still, as I have said, some remote trace of it in every tree that grows. Maybe occasionally – just occasionally – a tree grows that has not just the possibilities but the attributes – or some of them – that were there at the beginning. Another *Wudu*. There will be others, destined to remain undiscovered unless someone with a Maker's eye, a Maker's hand and a Maker's mind comes across it and unlocks that latent power."

"But what are we supposed to do with it?" Meg felt

a slight shiver of anxiety creep up her back. Being a Maker was harder to bear than she'd imagined.

"I doubt if there's an answer to that. A Maker doesn't have standing in our society. There's no pattern to follow, no expectation. Makers are unrecognized or misunderstood. The act of making has become mere construction, and wood is regarded as just another resistant material like stone, iron or glass.

"I think it's up to each Maker to decide how to use their own gift. I put all my practical skill into making the book, and since then I've concentrated on what the Crystal Eye can reveal to me about life, the past and the mysteries of the world. Only occasionally does it jolt me into practical action. You, I am sure, will always be a carver, and you'll always use Bolly-Bolly to enlighten you about problems here and now, even when he has some wisdom and experience, which he hasn't at the moment."

And neither have I, Meg thought, as she put him back in the bag. But I'm *learning*.

Another half an hour of walking and talking, and they reached the end of the ridge where the track sloped away in front of them, down into Halifax. Meg felt she had learned more this morning than ever before.

But learning was often like that; it didn't happen gradually, but all at once. She remembered when Mother taught her to knit (she said it was a more suitable activity for a lass then carving); she tried and tried but couldn't do it. Then suddenly, one day she could.

She felt glad about her own good fortune in meeting Dr. Challenor, then guilty, as her thoughts turned back to Father. How could she possibly feel happy while he was languishing down there? The sun lit up the hill behind the town, crowned with the iron frame of the beacon. When the fire was lit it sent news of momentous events from one hilltop to another. Momentous events were happening to Meg and those around her, but nobody would light a fire. Instead, if their rescue failed and her father was executed, his body would be hung on the beacon frame for all to see and the crows to peck.

The town was still in shadow. Shadowy deeds were planned down there. By the time the sun had passed over the town and lit up the other hillside, it would all be over – one way or the other. But which way?

There was no point in tormenting herself. She shook her head and followed Dr. Challenor down the track.

20

WAITING

When Meg and Dr. Challenor arrived at the smithy, Ned was helping Simon to his feet.

"He's just had another o' them visions." Ned pulled an axe from a large section of a tree that served Hal as a chopping block, and sat Simon down on it. He still looked a bit pale, but he wasn't shaking.

Meg was worried. Simon had warned her that his visions rarely came singly, but how long were they likely to go on for? She wished there was something she could do. Sitting down beside him, she started to brush the dirt from the floor off his clothes.

He gave her a thin smile. "It hasn't taken much out of me. I think I'm getting used to them again. This was the same as the last one – where the stag was chased over the water. Only this time the hounds had human faces – Sutcliffe, Womersley, the bailiff, the constable."

She took his hand and gave it a squeeze. "I wish we could stop them. I don't like the thought of you having to get used to them."

Dr. Challenor came in with a box, pulled up a barrel to Hal's anvil and took out his writing equipment.

Ned, apparently satisfied that Simon was on the mend, was rummaging in a pannier. "Hal an' Tom's gone to Womersley's with a couple of others to get Toby. They wasn't in no mood to be told no, I can tell you!" He held up a familiar dress and pulled it over his head. "I've just come back from the Cross, an' you'd scarce believe what's happened while we've been away."

Meg's pulse quickened. Was this good news or bad?

"We're all wanted now. We're all missin', so the bailiff thinks us three conspired to attack an' rob Sutcliffe an' Eastwood. An' on the basis o' that, he decides we robbed that gent at the fair an' all, then palmed his purse off on Jake. He gets a paper signed by the justice an' sets Jake free! That's why," he gave the dress a final tug over his belly, "I'm goin' to have to be Nan's sister again." He stuffed the padding of his false bosom inside the top and gave them the gap-toothed grin.

Then he saw what Dr. Challenor was doing and stared at him in amazement. "This ain't no time to write!"

"On the contrary," Dr. Challenor responded, without looking up. "You may be given to action, but do not underestimate the power of the pen." This had to be something to do with what Dr. Challenor had hinted at as he and Meg were walking. "I intend to masquerade as a court official. This is a letter from the Lord Chief Justice, requiring the authorities in Halifax to 'render all assistance to the bearer' – I need a name – er...Josiah Redgrove. That sounds sufficiently imposing – 'render all assistance to the bearer in his examination of the carriage, undertaking and pursuance of justice in the town hereinafter named, to wit Halifax, in the Manor of Wakefield, in the County of York, with particular regard to Gibbet Law.'" So Dr. Challenor was going to be somebody else too, though he didn't need different clothes to do it.

"Do you think they'll let you onto the platform?" Meg asked.

"I shall insist on it. There might be some

irregularity I can seize on and demand the execution be postponed, or I can make sure they take Toby's change of testimony seriously."

Meg watched the neat, black characters of the letter make their way across the paper, just like those in the book.

"But what about the seal?" Ned asked.

"I have a signet." Dr. Challenor held up a ring. "Do you think the local bailiff will know it's not that of the Lord Chief Justice? Don't get the wrong idea when you see me on the platform – I haven't suddenly become one of the enemy."

Ned gave a loud guffaw. "Good for you. I'd never ha' thought o' that." He pulled on the wig and plonked a mob cap on top of it.

Dr. Challenor finished the letter and sprinkled sand on to dry the ink. Then he folded it, dripped on melted wax and pressed the signet ring in to seal it.

"I'll repair to the Cock for breakfast," he said. "As befits a man of my station. I'll see what I can discover there, and maybe sow some seeds of doubt." He stood in front of Meg, put his hands on her shoulders and looked at her. "I won't say 'don't worry', because I know you will. What I will say, is don't let the worry extinguish the hope. If everything – or most things –

go according to plan, your father will be free in a matter of hours."

Ned was making last-minute adjustments to his costume.

"Nan's coming to stay with you," he said. "We'll send news as quick as we can."

Meg felt a moment's annoyance on top of her mounting frustration. She knew why her friends wanted to keep her hidden, but she'd already been in grave danger and survived; she wasn't helpless. She could sense Ned's and Dr. Challenor's excitement; they had plans to make, things to do, while she and Simon were supposed to stay here and wait. There had to be some way she could help with the rescue, but to do that she needed to be there, by the gibbet. The problem was she'd be recognized by those on the platform, unless... An idea came into her mind.

Simon was annoyed too. He was about to say something to Ned, but Meg dug him in the ribs. He half turned towards her and she put a finger to her lips. Ned was tying on a pair of dilapidated shoes.

"That's it," he said. "Let's all hope for the best o' luck." He gave them both a hug and left with Dr. Challenor.

Meg jumped down from the chopping block, ran to the pannier and delved inside.

"What are you...? Oh, of course!" Simon jumped down too and joined her.

"If Ned and Dr. Challenor are playing other parts, why can't we?" Meg said, holding a dark blue dress against herself. It was too big, so she cast it aside. Simon was finding other things, a bag of wigs, hats, boots and shoes. He pulled them out and laid them on the chopping block.

"Most of this stuff's too big," Meg said, discarding another dress.

Simon crammed a felt hat like a pudding basin on his head, leaving a fringe of hair round the edge. "Maybe it wouldn't matter if we were beggars – we'd just wear anything, wouldn't we?"

"But wouldn't we be run out of town as vagrants?"

"I expect the bailiff and his men have other things to think about today, and there'll be a huge crowd."

He found a shabby black coat that nearly covered him, and a pair of boots; worn, scuffed and gaping at the toe. Then, as well as the hat, he tied a filthy bandage over one eye.

Meg dived into the pannier again and brought out a red satin dress decorated with pink and white rosebuds. It had been beautiful and costly once, but now it was dirty, torn, rather smelly and half the rosebuds were missing.

"That's it!" Simon said. "Try it on."

Meg wasn't sure that she wanted to, but this wasn't the time to be too particular. She struggled into it and took a turn up and down the smithy. It had a fitted waist and frills and flounces down to the ground. At the neck there was a huge ruff that was a bit uncomfortable, but made it more difficult for people to see her face properly.

"Dirt," Meg said. "We need to be dirtier." She bent down and rubbed dust from the floor over her face and hands. "How do I look?" she asked.

"Different – apart from the hair. What about this?" Simon held out a ginger wig. "My hair's not quite that colour, but it might make you pass for my sister."

Meg liked the idea, if not the wig, and pulled it on.

Simon tucked a few stray wisps of her own hair under the edge, and stepped back. "That's good," he said. "You don't look like you at all. Even your mother wouldn't recognize you."

As they walked out of the smithy, Meg expected passers-by to denounce them as impostors. No one did. But when she saw Nan bustling down the street towards them, muttering to herself, Meg was sure they'd be found out. Nan glanced at them, but that was all; no second glance, no glint of recognition in her eye.

As they drew near the gibbet there were more people, and a growing sense of expectation in the air. It was surprisingly easy to merge into the crowd and become part of the throng. A rough fence had been put up a few feet away from the gibbet platform to stop people getting too close.

"We don't want to be too near the front," said Simon. "We'll get swallowed up and not see anything."

"There's a good spot." Meg pointed to a low wall that gave onto the gable end of a house at the other side of the street. "If we stand with our backs to it, nobody can push us from behind. And we can jump on the wall if we want to."

They walked over to the wall and sat on it. Now all they had to do was wait. And that would be harder than anything.

* * *

The space round the gibbet and the streets approaching it was filling up all the time. People appeared at the upper windows of nearby shops and houses. Meg could even see some people on the roof of the Cross, which stood out above the lower buildings.

Some of the vendors from the fair were here again. Meg could see the hot potato man at the other side of the platform. A pie seller came past with a large basket on her arm, shouting her wares.

"Execution pies. Buy yourself a 'heading pie specially made for the occasion."

She was making her way past them and Meg peered in the basket. Every pie had a pastry cutout of the gibbet on top.

"Hey, keep yer nose out ye little beggar," the seller said and made a slap at her. "No pay, no pie."

Meg was bewildered. All these people, and none of them knew Father at all. It didn't matter to them who was about to be beheaded; it was just a holiday, another excuse to eat a pie and have a drink. Nothing seemed real. It felt as if everybody else was in fancy dress too, as if they were all part of a big play, and when the blade came down and it was all over, Father would jump up and take a bow.

Except it wouldn't be like that. If Toby Gledhill

didn't change his mind, and the blade really did come down, then that would be the end. No jumping up. Father would be dead.

She moved closer to Simon and took hold of his arm.

"Do you think Hal will have Toby by now?" she asked. There might not be much point in asking, but it was so important that she couldn't think of anything else. Every time there was movement in the crowd she looked for the burly figure of Hal, only to be disappointed as the pie seller emerged, or a furious gentleman with no interest in the execution tried to go about his business.

"Hal won't let us down," Simon said. "Ned doesn't mean to show Toby till your father's on the platform, so he said. That way everybody notices, everybody sees and hears him. There's plenty of time."

Did he mean that? There was something a bit too hearty about the way he said it, as though he was trying to convince himself too. What if they couldn't find Toby, or he wouldn't change his testimony? Just for once Meg wished she really did have the kind of powers that some people thought witches had, and could put a spell on the bailiff, the bullock, the gibbet. Anything to save Father.

There was a general stirring in the crowd now. Meg stood up on the wall to see what the fuss was about. She could see a ladder sticking up, and a group of men pushing their way down the street, trying to look important. A guard by the fence raised his voice. "Make way there!" He pushed people back and opened a gate to let the men through.

There were three of them, and they went up the steps onto the platform. One man set the ladder up at the gibbet frame, while another emptied the contents of a sack he had been carrying onto the ground. The blade, shaped like a huge axe head, clanged onto the flagstones and a rope fell out with it. They had come to set up the gibbet. The third man on the platform was the constable, no doubt come to make sure the job was properly done.

Bolly-Bolly was restless. He wanted to see what was happening. Meg jumped down. There were slits in the skirts of the dress, so she was able to put her hand through and take him out of the bag underneath. She didn't think there was a risk. Nobody would be interested in a girl with a wooden figure.

Bolly-Bolly was in an awkward mood. He didn't approve of the way she was dressed. Or Simon. And why were they standing here doing nothing? He, Bolly-

Bolly, conqueror of demons, needed something to do.

Meg was in no mood to humour him.

If he wanted something to do he could find it for himself. She had enough to worry about without providing entertainment for bored and crotchety pieces of wood.

That was too much! She'd better be careful what she said, or he would go into a sulk for days. If she didn't appreciate his talents she could put him back in the bag now and manage on her own.

Well, she might just do that, seeing as he couldn't come up with...

Wait a minute... There were demons about – Meg could feel Bolly-Bolly sensing them – but they were quiet. He couldn't tell exactly where they were, but just let them try to start anything! It was a good job for Meg that he enjoyed fighting demons, otherwise he'd leave her to cope with them herself, after what she'd said about him.

Whatever concerns Meg had had about him after the incident in the clearing, Bolly-Bolly was certainly back to normal now.

A tolling bell brought her back to the reality in front of her. Did it mean that Father was on his way? She could see a bullock in the field behind the gibbet, standing patiently with its master while the rope from the peg was attached to its collar. Its owner looked nervous, pacing up and down, no doubt wishing that somebody else had been chosen for the task.

There were other signs that the time was near. The bailiff was there at the bottom of the steps, with Womersley. And a man with a bagpipe was tuning his drones. They were waiting, but they had the air of people who didn't expect to wait long. There was Dr. Challenor, standing slightly apart and looking important.

A movement in the crowd along the street in the direction of the gaol and the dull thump of a drum, announced the approach of the gibbet procession. What looked like a solid mass of people parted to make a way down the middle.

First came the drummer, the head of his drum covered with a cloth to muffle the sound. Behind him a priest, with what must be a bible clutched to his chest. Then Meg caught her first glimpse of Father, shackled between two of the constable's men. He was trying to walk upright and slowly, to the pace set by the drummer, but he was limping. Even from this distance his face looked drawn, and one eye was almost closed.

What had they done to him in gaol? Meg wanted

to yell, shout, scream, to let Father know that she was there, tell him not to give up hope. She couldn't do that, of course. She had to bottle up her feelings, because if she gave anything away then the whole plan might fail.

The clang of the church bell measured the party's progress. A hush fell over the watching crowd. It was like a religious procession, not the taking of an innocent man to his death. This was terrible. It made it seem as though God approved of it, and Meg was sure He didn't. Even Father seemed to go along with it, his mouth set firm and his chin thrust out, going to his death with dignity.

Then she saw a little knot of people at the back of the group. There was Mother, holding Robert, and Gaffer limping along with his arm round her. Meg brought her hand to her mouth to stop herself crying out and jumped down off the wall – she couldn't bear it. She should be there with them, not one of the crowd. Tears flowed now, and she couldn't prevent little moans escaping from her mouth, even though she bit her finger to try and stop them.

Simon put his arm round her and held her tightly.

"Do you want to go back to the smithy?" he whispered in her ear.

It was too late now. There were so many people Meg didn't think she'd be able to make her way through them. Not only that, it would be...disloyal. She couldn't desert Father, even if there was nothing she could do. When she thought how he must feel, then her own feelings were not that important. She had to be here, even if he never knew it. She shook her head and muffled a sob.

It seemed to be catching. Other people were crying too, and they had never seen Father before. But Meg wanted to be strong. Father was being strong; Mother and Gaffer were being strong and they didn't know that there was any possibility of rescue. Meg took a deep, shuddering breath, pulled away from Simon and climbed back onto the wall. She had to watch what was going on.

The procession reached the bottom of the platform. The drummer stepped to one side and the priest climbed the steps. They led Father up behind him and stood him in front of the block facing the crowd, while the piper struck up. Meg had heard the tune before, in church. It was one they sang a psalm to. She could even remember the words: "I will lay me down in peace, and sleep: for Thou, Lord, only makest me dwell in safety".

She looked over people's heads, scanning the streets for any sign of Hal. Simon had climbed onto the wall, and he was looking too. He was as anxious about Hal's absence as she was.

The bagpipes stopped, and the priest started to read, though she couldn't hear what he was saying. The guards turned Father round and made him kneel down and place his head on the block. Everything was in place for the blade to descend. Dr. Challenor watched from the back of the platform. Was he going to intervene?

A ripple in the crowd from the direction of the smithy caught Meg's attention. Here was Hal at last! He was forcing his way through the crowd, dragging someone else with him. A wave of relief swept over her.

"Hal's here!" she couldn't prevent herself shouting.

Simon grinned. "And not a moment too soon."

It wasn't until Hal was quite near, only a few feet from the wall, that Meg realized with horror that it wasn't Toby he had with him, but Tom, his apprentice. Hal's face was a mask of blank despair. Tom was white-faced and breathless.

Ned emerged from the crowd, pushing his way towards the new arrivals. They recognized him, because they'd seen him in disguise last night.

"What's the matter?" Ned asked.

"He...he says..." Tom struggled to get his message out. "He says Toby's dead!"

THE ADVERSARY

For a moment the world stood still. Of all the things that could possibly have gone wrong, Meg had never thought of this. Now there was no point in restraining herself. "My father is innocent!" she shouted. "He would never steal cloth from anybody."

Ned looked at her with disbelief. "He ain't your father, he..." Then he looked closer. "I knows that dress, an' that wig. An' Simon too! You don't intend to be left out, do you? Come on!"

Everything happened at once. Hal went forging through the crowd towards the gibbet, with Ned shouting and waving his hands above his head. Meg followed in their wake. Simon came too, causing as much noise and confusion as he could. Everybody needed to be aware of the disturbance.

"Stop! John Lumb is innocent. We 'ave hevidence!" Ned sounded more like Nan than ever. His voice was louder than Meg's, and drowned out the measured tones of the bailiff, who was reading the charge. The bailiff paused. Heads turned. Sutcliffe and the constable, standing at the foot of the platform, looked at each other. The solemn mood that had been carefully created, vanished, and people began to mutter.

Then, in his eagerness, Ned gave one push too many. A burly arm came out and stopped him in his tracks, causing Meg to bump into him. His wig shot off and disappeared in a mass of bodies.

"Here, what's this?" said the man the arm belonged to. "He's not a woman!"

Sutcliffe was only a few yards away at the bottom of the steps.

"Hold him! He's a wanted man," he said, then, looking up at the bailiff, "Get on with it, man! We have business to finish." Those final words were meant for Meg too. He turned his eyes on her with a look of cold hatred that sent her weak at the knees.

Dr. Challenor stepped forward, determined to make the most of the disruption to the proceedings. "If there is evidence I demand you hear it, by the authority of the Lord Chief Justice. A man's life is at stake."

Ned struggled to try and free himself from his captor. Meg heard Toby's name mentioned, but the burly fellow had his arm across Ned's face and all his words were muffled.

The bailiff looked nervous and undecided. He started to read again, then stopped as Hal tore planks from the barrier, broke through and made for the steps, causing even more confusion as the men guarding them tried to stop him.

Sutcliffe gave a furious roar, and moved away out of sight round the corner of the platform. There was something about the way he was moving – quickly, with a sense of purpose – that alarmed Meg. She squirmed through the gap in the fence that Hal had made, and ran along the bottom of the platform, round behind it. She could see Sutcliffe striding towards the drover with his bullock, waiting patiently for the signal to drive forward and pull out the peg.

Sutcliffe's intention hit her like a blow to the stomach. He was going to take the law into his own hands. Whatever happened with the interrupted course of events, he was going to make sure that the execution took place.

No one above her seemed to have noticed. She shouted as loudly as she could, jumping up so she could be seen from the platform, but there was too much noise for her voice to be heard, and nobody saw her. Everything was going wrong. Why didn't somebody look up and see what Sutcliffe was doing?

Bolly-Bolly chose this of all moments to demand her attention. She still had him out of the bag, clutching him tightly, and he was struggling in her hands. She felt like throwing him at somebody's head; maybe that would draw their attention to what Sutcliffe was about. But – she should know by now – it was never a good idea to ignore Bolly-Bolly. If anyone could rescue the situation he could, though how she had no idea.

He was very excited.

Come on, concentrate, concentrate!

Meg slackened her grasp and looked at him, letting her own power merge with his.

No clear image, just swirling green.

Sutcliffe had nearly reached the bullock.

Now it was taking shape – a tree, the swirling, wind-tossed branches of a tree. The one she could see from the cottage, the tree she had carved on the bottom of the gibbet frame, with the setting sun in its branches.

Sutcliffe had his hand on the rope and gave it a tug. He wasn't a bullock. It would take more than that to dislodge the peg.

Tree. Wood. Wudu. The gibbet had once been a tree; a sturdy oak growing in the forest. It had been cut down, with others. Some had gone to make ships. It had been selected to be the frame for the town gibbet. Itself cut down by men, it was to be the means of cutting men down.

Sutcliffe tried again, but he wasn't strong enough. People were running towards him now, shouting, trying to stop him. He took no notice and strode up to the drover.

The gibbet. Once a tree. Deep in its heartwood it can dimly recall the sap rising up its trunk and along its branches. It remembers the stirring of its roots and the sensation of growth – limbs stretching up, supporting a dense canopy of branches and leaves. Stirred by the memory, it imagines itself a tree again – the twist and flex of living grain, not the crack and splinter of dead wood. Green oak, live oak. It feels the shuddering surge of life run through it and reaches for the sky again.

The argument with the drover was brief. Sutcliffe grabbed his stick and gave the bullock a hard thwack.

The startled animal plunged forward. The peg flew out. The blade fell.

And stopped.

A gasp went up from the crowd.

Bolly-Bolly kept his focus on the tree. Meg stepped away from the wall of the platform until she could see the top of the gibbet. The two uprights had grown thicker and were leaning towards each other. Their texture was rougher, obliterating the names and scrawling on their surface. The grooves that allowed the blade to travel down had become no more than fissures in bark. Meg's tree was now incorporated in this greater tree which was both new and old.

The block that carried the gibbet blade was caught in branches that were growing, snaking round it and enmeshing it in an impenetrable green tracery. The instrument of death had come to life.

Meg shook as all her pent-up anxiety left her. This wasn't part of the plan. This was something only she could have done. Bolly-Bolly, with his deep secrets, had enabled her to stop the gibbet blade in its tracks. Wiping away tears of relief that welled in her eyes, she looked up into the branches again – and caught her breath.

Something different was happening to the gibbet tree. It had stopped growing. A branch that Meg had just watched putting forth leaves was now shrivelled and dead. As quickly as it had flourished, the new growth was dying back.

A sharp reaction from Bolly-Bolly alerted Meg. He was angry and puzzled. Then, with sudden clarity, as though he were lit up, Meg picked out one of the crowd thronging at the town side of the gibbet. It was Jake, and he was holding something she recognized in his hands – the eyeball. But how did Jake come to have it? And did he have some magic that he could channel through it to defeat her – and Bolly-Bolly's – purpose?

The twin trunks of the tree groaned and creaked as they straightened themselves, trying once more to take on the shape and form of the gibbet frame. The branches imprisoning the blade cracked and snapped as they broke away.

Jake raised his head, and looked across the space between himself and Meg. Their eyes met, and his intense, piercing gaze held hers. With a sickening shock she recognized it. For a moment, she had enjoyed the jubilation of what she thought was success, but now it all drained away. Now she knew how Jake came to have the eyeball. She was transported for a moment back to the clearing in the wood. She was staring into the eyes of the adversary. But how could Jake and the adversary be one and the same? Jake had been in prison when she had faced it before. This wasn't the time or place to resolve such a contradiction.

She felt herself being lulled into a weary acceptance of defeat. She couldn't let that happen. She tore her eyes away from the adversary and returned her fierce, undivided attention to Bolly-Bolly. His previous magic was being undone. She tried desperately to get him to counter Jake's magic. He *must* have more power than Jake could summon up. What was wrong?

"It's *yours*!" Bolly-Bolly's voice burst in on her. She had never seen him in such distress.

"The demon has the eyeball, but it's using your magic. I can't fight it!"

Meg was gripped by panic. The gibbet hadn't quite returned to its normal stark outline, but it was nearly there. In a few moments the grooves would be aligned again and the blade would continue its interrupted fall. Tension crackled in the air. She was doing no good down here; she must get onto the platform.

She put Bolly-Bolly back in the bag and ran round the corner of the platform, and nearly bumped into Simon coming the other way without his hat and boots.

"There you are! What's—"

"Quickly! I need to get up there."

Simon didn't wait for an explanation; he took her foot in his cupped hands and hoisted her up the wall. Her fingers scrabbled for a hold on the top edge. She felt Simon's shoulders under her now; another boost and she was scrambling onto the flagstones that paved the platform.

Sutcliffe was back already. He and Dr. Challenor were at each other's throats, while the bailiff and the constable were trying to keep them apart. The priest stood at the back with his bible clutched to his chest like a protective shield.

Father was still kneeling at the base of the gibbet – held there by one of the constable's men – arms tied behind him, neck on the block, his blindfold in place. Meg could see him struggling. He could have no idea what had happened, what all the noise was and what the strange reaction of the crowd meant.

Was the adversary going to win? She had defeated it in the clearing, but now that it had added her magic to its own, there seemed to be nothing to stop it succeeding. Meg looked at the gibbet blade teetering on the edge of falling. She had failed. Bolly-Bolly had failed.

All the fight went out of her. She couldn't bear to look any more. Her eyes stared blankly over the men struggling on the platform, over the sea of faces below her, to the brook and the hill beyond.

The brook! That repeated vision of Simon's, the one he couldn't find any explanation for – what had happened? He had seen the stag being pursued to the water, but once it had made the far bank it was safe. Suddenly, it made sense. There was one more chance. She threw herself down beside her father.

"Run, Father, run!" she screamed, before the constable's man hauled her away.

Her voice cut through the confusion. Hal heard what she said, broke away from the three men who were trying to hold him down, and bounded up the steps. He swept the constable's man aside with one hand and held back the bailiff with the other. Sutcliffe sprang at Hal, but he hadn't beaten Dr. Challenor, who grabbed him from behind, dragged him away from the gibbet and off the edge of the platform.

Meg had her shut-knife out and cut the bonds

binding Father's wrists as he staggered to his feet. He tore off his blindfold and looked wildly around him. Then, with two strides and a leap he was off the back of the platform. He was running almost before he hit the ground. Sutcliffe struggled to his feet and tried to cut him off, but Father brushed him aside as he sped past.

"Don't let him get across the brook," Sutcliffe roared. "A guinea to the man who can catch him!" It reminded Meg of the last time she had watched Father being pursued.

She could see a dozen or so – mainly young men – rushing after Father, but for most of the crowd this was unexpected entertainment. They had come to see a beheading, but they had witnessed the inexplicable transformation of the gibbet – surely some kind of vision – and now they were seeing a life-or-death race. And, if Father was caught, they might still have their beheading.

Father himself had told her the story years ago. The Running Man. It came flooding back to her. The other side of the water was outside the township, and that meant safety. She had never been quite sure why that should be, but listening to the people around her, she knew now. Gibbet Law didn't apply across the boundary on the other side of the brook. Once there, they couldn't touch you.

Father was more than halfway there now. Most of his pursuers had given up, but the two leaders were closing on him, and he was tiring. He would have to summon up some extra energy from somewhere. She didn't dare watch but found it impossible not to. Father was pumping his arms, forcing his legs to keep going. She willed him on with all her strength.

The two leading pursuers had almost reached him. Meg's heart was in her mouth. Then one turned and, slowing slightly, brought his knee up into the other's groin. The man doubled up, clutching himself. But, as he fell, he reached out and grabbed the other one's leg. They landed in a heap, hitting out at each other. They were obviously prepared to lose everything rather than share a guinea.

Father glanced back and slackened his pace. He brought his hand up to his side, feeling a stitch, no doubt, and slowed to a walk. He only had a short distance to go. Nobody was going to catch him now.

Then, on the other side of the brook, Meg saw something that made her blood run cold. Jake was standing on the bank. How on earth had he managed to get there? She glanced at the section of the crowd where she had last seen him. People had moved a bit, but there was no mistaking that figure – he was still there!

They couldn't both be Jake. One of them must be someone in disguise, like herself, though she was at a loss to know why. Whoever it was down by the brook, he was determined to stop Father crossing over. He had come through the water and was advancing, while Father, who had already run down the field and was in an exhausted state anyway, backed off, moving further away from the brook.

Meg was with a whole crowd of people making their way down the field, but some were running ahead. Dr. Challenor was moving faster than she could ever have imagined. Simon was there, with Hal at his shoulder, making it obvious in his own way that anyone who still fancied trying to claim a guinea would have him to reckon with.

It was clear that they were going to reach Father first. The thin Jake-figure stopped, looked at Father, then at the advancing runners. Jake must have realized that he couldn't deal with all of them. With a cry of rage he plunged into the brook, waded back to the other side and started to toil up the hill. He looked tired, pulling himself up the steep slope using thick tufts of grass and straggly bushes.

Another figure of the same size and build emerged from a small clump of windswept trees and joined him. Two Jakes, climbing side by side.

Meg reached Dr. Challenor, still out of breath.

"There you have the answer," he said, as if she'd asked him the question that was in her mind. "One Jake in prison while his demon double roamed free to rob Eastwood of your eyeball and torment you. The adversary."

The two figures moved closer and closer, merging together until they were one. And Meg heard again the strange shriek that she knew would haunt her dreams for a long time to come.

Father stood beside the brook, looking down at the rushing water and the stony bottom. He took one more glance back. The crowd were in a mood for celebration. In the end, they were glad Father had escaped. He put one foot in the water, then the other, tottered across with the very last of his strength, and fell to his knees on the other side. A shout went up, then another, and soon the whole crowd was cheering.

Except for two. Glancing back, Meg saw Sutcliffe and Womersley, standing to one side, deep in conversation. They bore their disappointment in very different ways. Sutcliffe's face was red with anger at having his plans thwarted. He stamped a foot on the ground and flung his arms about, jabbing a finger in Womersley's chest to emphasize a point. Womersley stood straight and stiff, his face white and expressionless. Meg thought of Toby and shivered.

She turned round as she heard Ned's voice calling her. He wasn't in disguise any more. He'd pulled the dress off, leaving him in shirt and pantaloons. And he had Mother and Gaffer with him. They were smiling. Mother was pale, and her eyes were red. She looked at Meg with a mixture of relief and amazement. What had Ned been telling her?

"What's a goin' on up there?" Ned was peering up the hillside, a hand shielding his eyes from the light.

Meg followed his gaze: some kind of struggle, a whirl of arms and legs, two figures tussling and wrestling on the ground, sliding down the hill as they did so. It was Simon and Jake. Simon must have followed Jake up the hill – but why? Did he think he had something to prove to himself, or even to her? Meg felt both anxious and annoyed at him.

The two reached a flatter part of the hillside above the steep lower slope. Despite being so much smaller, Simon managed to haul himself on top and sit astride Jake's chest. All Jake's strength seemed to have gone. Simon pinned his arms down with his knees and appeared to be searching through his clothing.

Simon found what he was looking for, and held it up. The eyeball. Meg felt a pang of guilt at having misread Simon's intentions. He wanted to take advantage of Jake's weakened state to take back the eyeball so that Jake's demon double could no longer use it against her.

She was about to say something to Dr. Challenor, when a cry from Simon drew her eyes back to the hill. The eyeball was no longer in his hands, it was up in the air. Meg watched it rise and fall, then bounce and roll down the hillside. Jake seemed as if he had shed a burden. With a surge, he flung Simon off and sent him tumbling and scrambling down the hill after the eyeball, while he continued upwards with renewed energy.

The eyeball reached the bottom first, and stopped just short of the brook. Simon arrived seconds later, sprawling on the grass. He picked himself up, looking shaken but unhurt, and stared at the eyeball. Meg crossed the water and saw what had caught his attention; flames were licking across the surface, darting from one eye to another. Then there was a small explosion, and sparks shot into the air.

Meg grabbed Simon and pulled him away. She could feel a searing heat from the eyeball, which became unbearably bright. In moments, it had burned away to a small pile of white ash.

Dr. Challenor had joined them. "The adversary would rather destroy the eyeball than let it return to you. He is certainly less powerful without it, and probably thinks you are too, though I doubt if it's the kind of power you would want to use."

Further along the bank, Father was partly sitting up now, resting on his elbows. Meg pulled off her wig and ran towards him. Father saw her coming. He leaned forward and she flung herself into his arms.

He didn't say anything, but he held her to him, and she could feel the rise and fall of his chest. For a moment all the upheaval of the past few days slipped away. She felt as if she was a little girl again, and her father was the strongest man in the world.

22

PARTING

Simon played the final chord, and Dilly-Lal's clattering feet came to a halt. Meg took Simon's hand and raised it in the air. They made a good team. Clapping and cheering rang round the Cross's yard. The locals hadn't forgotten the performance on fair night, and wanted more. Now that Father was safe, Meg was happy to oblige. Nan was taking a collection "for the Lumb family, to alleviate their 'ardship", so she said.

They had been assured by the bailiff – under the watchful eye of "Josiah Redgrove" – that Father wouldn't be rearrested if he came back across the brook. The evidence would be looked at afresh in the light of the unexplained death of the chief witness, and the testimony of those who had seen John Lumb travelling towards home with his own piece on fair day. So it had been arranged that the family would stay at the Cross overnight before returning to Heptonstall.

Ned and Simon had decided to stay too, which pleased Meg, because she wanted to say goodbye properly. She had thought Simon would go back to York to continue his apprenticeship with Dr. Challenor, but Dr. Challenor said the time wasn't right and had ridden off before anyone could question his false identity.

Suddenly, the applause died and the audience went quiet. Heads turned to the yard entrance. Someone was there; someone who wasn't part of the celebrations. The Reverend Nathaniel Eastwood stepped into the yard, his shoulders hunched, glowering like a giant crow.

"So the image magic continues," he said. "And in full public view! Is this directed against Patience Sutcliffe too? Will she find herself dancing and unable to stop until she falls in a dead swound upon the ground? Or is this aimed at some other poor unfortunate who has attracted your spite?"

For a moment, Meg didn't understand what he was talking about, but when she did it was so ridiculous and far from the mark that she felt like laughing. How on earth could he think that there was anything sinister in Dilly-Lal's dancing? But one look at his hard, narrow stare convinced her that he did.

"And the rest of you." His eyes swept across the assembly. "You have been watching what you no doubt considered innocent entertainment. But let me tell you, there is nothing innocent about *en-ter-tain-ment*" – he spat the word out as though it had a bad taste – "particularly from rogues and vagabonds such as these." He flung his hand out contemptuously towards Ned and Simon. "You would have been better served at home on your knees begging the Lord's forgiveness for your sins." Some of the onlookers made their goodbyes and shuffled awkwardly across the yard. Others looked abashed and uncomfortable, unwilling to meet Eastwood's unforgiving gaze.

The landlord appeared at the door of the inn.

"What are you doing here?" he said, scowling at the minister. "We're no lovers of Puritans at this inn, with your long faces and your dry throats. Get out of my yard!"

Eastwood tried to look defiant, but the landlord was big and used to dealing with difficult customers. He took one step towards him, and the minister slunk away, giving Meg a poisonous parting glance.

"You may think you've escaped the law," he said. "But not God's law. God is not mocked. You will be punished for your wickedness, mark my words."

"Never mind him," the landlord said, putting an arm round Meg's shoulder. "You don't take no notice o' them sort."

The landlord might not, but Meg knew there were those who did. There might not be many truly devout Puritans in the village, but they were influential. Just minutes ago she had felt happier than she had for months, thinking that all her troubles were over. Maybe they weren't. What was she going to do?

She ran across the yard to the stables.

"I'm going up to the hayloft," she said to Simon. "Don't come after me." She hoped he wouldn't be offended, but she needed to be alone.

She climbed up the ladder, threw herself down on the hay and stared up at the roof through a mist of tears. She thought about what she had been through over the past few days. One of the things that had kept her going during all the fear and hardship, was the thought that once it was over, once Father was free and the Sutcliffes discredited, they would all be together again, and life would go on as before.

But that wasn't to be. Her life in Heptonstall could

never be the same again. She had become the accused, and the minister certainly believed her guilty. Even more frightening, maybe Patience herself did too. Maybe the accusations would continue, even with Mr. Sutcliffe in prison or hanged. And it wouldn't stop there. Anything that went awry in the village would be laid at her door, and when Eastwood had enough so-called evidence he'd lay a charge against her. Of that she was absolutely sure. There was only one thing to do.

Meg jumped up, swarmed down the ladder and ran across the yard, ignoring Simon's questioning looks. Mother and Father had been watching events in the yard from the open doorway, and now they were sitting in a corner of the barroom talking quietly.

She only hesitated for a moment, then summoned up all her determination and thrust out her chin – she wasn't her father's daughter for nothing.

"I'm going with Ned and Simon," she said.

Mother was distraught. She tried to change Meg's mind, saying she needed her help, telling her they and their friends would look after her and she'd be safe.

Father was quiet, and that was worse. His face was drawn and pale. There were bruises and half-healed cuts on his face, and his wrists were red raw where the manacles had chafed. But looking into his eyes, Meg could see the same glint that had always been there. He had been shockingly treated and taken to the brink of death, but he hadn't been defeated. What was more, he understood.

He shifted his position on the bench and pulled his back straight against the wooden panelling behind.

"We have friends," he said, turning to Mother. "But we also have enemies, and there are those who go whichever way the wind blows. All villages are like that. And you just need one enemy like Eastwood. He won't rest until he has Meg on trial for witchcraft."

"But why does she have to go travelling the fairs?" Mother was clutching at straws now. "She could stay with her Aunt Lizzie. She'd be glad of the help with the family she's got."

Father gave her a long look. "Being an unpaid nursemaid and housekeeper for Lizzie is no life for her. If she has to leave, then..."

He stopped, fighting to keep his feelings under control. He was upset. He was having to let go. He knew she could look after herself, and that Simon and Ned were the most reliable and trustworthy of friends. Even so, it was hard for him. She would grow away from him no matter how she might try not to. They shouldn't be forced to part like this because, in truth, neither of them was ready for it. He took her hand and squeezed so hard it hurt.

With her other hand she opened the drawstring of her bag. There was something she had just remembered. She rummaged around until she felt her fingers snag on it – the flower Simon had given her on the gibbet platform. She pulled it out and held it up; it was dull and wilted now.

"Cinquefoil," she said. "It brings good luck and justice – protection and defence too. It seems to have worked for you if not for me." She wound it round Father's little finger.

Parting was difficult, as Meg knew it would be. But, after all the tears and heart-wringing, Mother, Father and Gaffer had set off west towards Heptonstall. A little later, Ned, Simon and Meg had gone the other way. They'd missed Pendle fair, so Ned, whose knowledge of the fairs was unrivalled, decided they would head for Wakefield.

They were clear of Halifax now, in the valley bottom, just over the bridge and about to face the long haul up the hill. The road cut diagonally across the slope. It was still very steep, but the pony was strong and patient.

"The company", as Ned insisted on calling them, "now there are three of us", were sitting on the box at the front of the cart, with their possessions under the canvas tilt behind. All their lives had changed, but Meg's most of all. As they neared the top of the slope, she turned round for a last look at the place that had been the scene of such strange and alarming events.

She'd never seen Halifax from this side before. It looked more spread out. It was cloudy, but she could just make out the shape of the gibbet on the edge of town. It looked small and insignificant from here. You couldn't tell what it was unless you knew. Her gaze travelled up the slope beyond, dotted with farms and other buildings as far as she could see. The tenterframes she had passed on her way into town now appeared as tiny dots of colour against the bright green of early summer grazing. If she knew exactly where it was, she could probably pick out Edgar Womersley's farm. The road she could see snaking up to Roils Head went past it.

Somewhere on that road, probably out of sight by now, the rest of her family were on their way home without her. She tried to imagine what the cottage would be like. They could throw out her mattress, so there'd be more room – until Robert grew too big for his cot. But there'd be no Meg to look after him, no Meg to whirl the wool dry or card it, no Meg to come running in from the graveyard and be told off for staying out too long.

"Thinking of home?" Simon asked.

"Yes."

"I still think of home – sometimes."

"Have you ever been back?"

"No. I sent a message once, but I don't know if it got there."

"But we'll come back here, won't we?"

"O' course we will," Ned reassured her. "Twice a year at least. You'll meet your folks, an' they'll see you can manage without 'em, an' you'll see they can manage without you. Times change an' we all get on with our lives. Everythin' changes." A ray of sunlight broke from behind a cloud. "Includin' the weather. That's what it's like to be one o' the travellin' folk. Every day's different."

It was something Meg would have to get used to. She turned her back on the view behind her and fixed her eye on the road ahead; the Wakefield road, heading east.

Author's Glossary

Some of the words in *Woodenface* have fallen out of use since the seventeenth century, or are regional words, so may not be familiar to modern readers.

ardent spirit – alcoholic spirit with a fiery taste

beck – stream

blunderbuss – gun with a flared barrel, firing many balls or slugs

card – to comb out fleece until it is free of tangles and ready for spinning

clinchpoop – term of contempt. Thought to be from someone who "clinched" (put the bolts in) the "poop" (back part) of a ship – a very lowly job

clough – narrow, steep-sided valley running into a bigger stream

coney – rabbit

gibbet – usually a gallows for hanging people, but the Halifax Gibbet was a beheading instrument like the French guillotine, except that the blade was a large axe head

ginnel – narrow alleyway

grubbing up – digging up by the roots

hedge-witch – a woman (usually) whose spells were likely to be based on plants, herbs and old folklore. Often looked down on by the local community

jogtrot – slow, easy-going

kersey – coarse cloth woven in "pieces". A piece was about one metre wide and thirteen metres long

king's evil, the – popular name for the disease scrofula (tuberculosis of the neck), because people believed it could be cured by the king's touch. One of the symptoms was purple swellings on the neck

lamper – someone who hunts rabbits at night with a lamp

lodestone – piece of magnetic oxide of iron used as a magnet

mazed – stupefied, bewildered

motion – puppet show

motion-man – puppeteer

mountebank – (literally "mount-on-bench") a quack. Somebody who stood up and sold useless remedies by being a convincing talker and showman

ostler – someone who looked after horses at an inn

pattens – overshoes that raised your feet up out of the mud and dirt

physic – medical treatment

playboard – horizontal board at the front of a puppet booth, where the action takes place

quartern loaf – loaf of bread made from a quartern (quarter of a stone – approximately 1.6kg) of flour

rake-hell – a thorough scoundrel

sack, bottle of – white wine imported from Spain

sett – large cobblestone

settle – long bench with a high back

shovelboard – game in which a coin is knocked by the hand along a highly-polished board with lines marked across it. The aim is to get the coin to stop between sets of lines

showcloth – decorated cloth hanging at the front of a puppet booth

shut-knife – knife where the blade shuts away for safety

sneck – door latch

snicket – narrow alleyway

sway-cleek – hook at the end of a flat, iron rod fixed to the side of a fireplace, which can be swung back and forth across the open fire. A pot or kettle would be hung from it

swound – fainting fit

tabor – small drum

tenterfield – field where tenterframes (see below) were put

tenterframe – hooked frame where dyed cloth was stretched to dry. The phrase "on tenterhooks" comes from this – when you are "stretched" and tense, waiting for something to happen

varlet – rogue

GUS GRENFELL has had many jobs in his life, including being a building society director, a market researcher, a folk musician, and a teacher working with school refusers and adults with learning disabilities. He has had many short stories and poems published, as well as an adult novel. *Woodenface* is his first novel for younger readers.

Gus lives with his wife Tessa – who is a weaver – three cats and a dog, on the Isle of Arran off the west coast of Scotland. He previously lived in the Yorkshire Pennines, where *Woodenface* is set, and ran a smallholding raising cattle, sheep, goats, pigs, poultry – and six children.

For more mysterious and compelling tales
log on to
www.fiction.usborne.com